TU'VER

CONQUERED WORLD: BOOK THREE

ELIN WYN

CLOCK
WALK
PUBLISHING

TU'VER

"ARGH!"
Sylor had stealthily waited in a corner, unnoticed as Axtin passed him by in the mess hall. The resulting sound he had made startled Axtin to the point of nearly dropping his tray.

I hid a smile and watched as Axtin 'threatened' Sylor and Sylor returned the threat with a compliment about Leena.

It was surprisingly entertaining.

We found ourselves eating together more often, the two teams that had infiltrated the Xathi ship to rescue Leena and the other humans. Sylor was interesting to listen to when he relaxed. A match for Axtin in the bravado department, almost a match for me in games of skill, and a match for some of the humans in terms of demented humor. And Karzin was a Valorni version of Vrehx, just much louder.

Two weeks had passed since the rescue, and tensions were high. The Xathi had been on edge since our infiltration of their ship, and it had forced us to be on edge ourselves.

Axtin turned his attention back to the table. "Duvest only has so much room for the refugees. We're about maxed out here as well. With the Xathi raiding everything that moves including the plants, what are we supposed to do?"

Vrehx shook his head. This had been the topic at hand for the last eight days, ever since Thribb told the Captain that our ship's system couldn't handle this many people for much longer. With nearly a hundred extra digestive systems using the facilities, our recycling systems, compromised as they were due to our crash on this strange world, were taxed to the limit.

With a heavy breath, Vrehx looked at Axtin, opened his mouth…and shut it again with a shrug. "I don't know. We've been able to keep pathways to Duvest and Einhiv open, and Sk'lar's team has found a set of tunnels that lead to Fraga…but since Fraga's been destroyed, the tunnels are essentially useless." He looked at his plate, moving his food around with his knife, then, apparently tired with eating, pushed his plate away and stood up. "I don't know, Axtin. I just don't know."

It was Daxion that spoke up, stopping Axtin from saying something undoubtedly brash. "We'll find a way, we always do."

Vrehx gave him a thankful nod and paced around the mess hall. The idea that we had brought the Xathi to this world and caused them to be targeted by one of the worst threats in the galaxy weighed on him heavily, as it did all of us.

Daxion and Sakev bid us a good evening and left. It was their turn for patrol and they wanted to get a few hours of sleep before they went out. That left Axtin, myself, and the pacing Vrehx to sit in the mess hall.

Axtin looked at me and asked. "And?"

Slightly confused, I nodded at him and arched my eyebrow.

"You've been quiet, which isn't anything new with you, but even you join in the conversation when it involves work. So…what's on your mind?"

I opened my mouth to answer but was interrupted by Vrehx sitting down. He motioned for me to continue and I did. "I've simply been trying to work some things out. I've been thinking about our current situation with the refugees, the Xathi, and our munitions."

"Oh? What about our munitions?" Axtin asked.

Trust him to pick up on anything involving his weapons.

"We've blown through about ten percent of our supply in the months since we crashed. That means we'll be out of ammo within a year based on the way the Xathi have been acting lately."

"Koso!" Axtin swore.

"I've been thinking about how to conserve them, but it would involve more of us in close combat. I'll be honest with you, I'm not particularly fond of the idea of getting close to the Xathi. Not all of us have the tough skin of the Valorni or a Skotan's scales," I said as I pointed at Vrehx.

He nodded and lightly flexed his scales into view, then smiled. "So, if things come down to it, we'll figure out which ones are better for hand-to-whatever combat and which ones are better at shooting, then we'll adjust."

Axtin smiled, flexed his muscles, and winked at me. "Don't worry Tu'ver, I'll protect you from the big, bad bugs. I'll just smash them all to pieces with my hammer."

At my chuckle, the other two laughed.

"Didn't realize you were developing a sense of humor," Axtin cracked.

The assassin inside of me, who had suppressed his

emotions for so long and expected others to do the same took umbrage.

But I had observed my crewmates, these other species, for a long time now. There was apparently something therapeutic about sharing humor.

We spent the next thirty or so minutes talking about everything and nothing, mostly nothing.

Oddly, it felt good to be included, to be part of the group. I had been the last one to join the crew, and although we had been around one another for almost a year, it had always been a professional relationship based strictly on stopping the Xathi.

I wasn't the only one thinking of the changes. "Do you two think we would have done this if we hadn't come here?" Axtin grabbed the last of the food from my plate.

"Done what?" Vrehx sipped his drink.

"*This.* This whole conversation where we sit here in the midst of a war, talk, do more than just tolerate one another."

Vrehx and I looked at one another, both of us apparently sharing the same look on our face because Axtin failed miserably at stifling a laugh. Another round of laughter ended with Axtin wiping tears from his eyes and Vrehx trying to catch his breath.

It felt...nice to let go.

Before I could stop myself, I took a deep breath, then struggled for the right words.

"What is it?" Vrehx asked.

Void. I wasn't a child. I barged straight ahead. "I'm not quite sure how to broach this subject, but I was wondering about your relationships with the human women."

"What about them?" Axtin raised his eyebrows.

"How is it that you've found a way to make them work? What I mean is, how do you look past the difference in species?"

Both looked at me, visibly trying to hide their grins. I regretted opening my mouth. I should never have asked these two fools this question.

It was Axtin that broke the silence first. "You like Mariella." It was a statement, and the lilt of his voice suggested that he was amused by the idea. "I knew there was something a little *special* about the way you looked at her, especially when you carried her."

"You did seem to take to her right away. You even ignored my orders," Vrehx added.

I looked at him in shock. "I'm sorry, Commander, but I do not remember you giving me an order."

"You were a little preoccupied." He turned to Axtin with a knowing look on his face. "You know? I think he was the first one to fall for one of the women."

"I think you're right. Our little Tu'ver was the first to fall in love. Aww."

They broke out into another round of laughter while I sat there. Could they be right? Did I 'fall' for Mariella right away?

Vrehx stopped laughing and put his hand on my shoulder. "I'm sorry, we don't mean to make you feel bad." I must have looked particularly dour, but he continued. "To answer your original question, once I got used to Jeneva's...personality...the fact that she's human didn't matter to me."

Axtin chimed in with a grin. "Yeah, her *personality* sure won you over. She's got a nice *personality* when she walks past." He laughed and ducked as Vrehx threw a gentle Skotan punch.

Maybe not so gentle.

"At least he's being complimentary," I said.

Vrehx turned back to me. "Jeneva's been good for me. I still want to defeat the Xathi, but now it's because I want to save her, us, and whoever else is out there from the Xathi. I want revenge, don't get me wrong, but that's not what drives me anymore, and that makes me feel good. She makes me feel good."

"Vrehx has a point." Axtin leaned forward, his smile still there, but voice serious. "Jeneva has been good for him, and Leena has been unbelievable for me. I wish to be worthy of her. I know that she's temperamental. I never really know if she's going to kiss me, kick me, or kill me, but that's what adds to our relationship. She'd be a fantastic Valorni."

"That she would," Vrehx agreed.

They were right. The women *had* changed them, and for the better.

Axtin's training was more controlled, less chaotic. Even his actions during patrol were more calculated, as if he wanted to make sure he did his job to the best of his ability.

Vrehx was calmer, less stringent about the rules and more willing to adapt to his team instead of trying to make us adapt to him.

What had Mariella done to me?

I'd always been calculated, 'slow' according to the old Axtin. I'd always been deliberate in my actions. None of that had changed, nor could I imagine it would.

So, what had Mariella done to me except make me feel a sense of separation when we were apart and a sense of joy when we were together?

Not sure about my own feelings, I thanked the two of them and excused myself.

Perhaps it was time to bury the assassin that Tu'ver had been.

And find a way to enter into a partnership with Mariella.

MARIELLA

"**D**o human men look strange to you now?"
I turned my head at the sound of Jeneva's voice, even though the question wasn't directed at me. She sat on top of a black storage crate, her back pressed against the wall and her head resting lazily on her shoulder to look at my sister.

Leena thought for a moment before a wicked grin spread across her face.

"Human men have always looked strange to me," she quipped. I giggled from my spot on the floor, my back pressed against the end of the same crate that Jeneva sat on. Jeneva threw her head back and laughed a full belly laugh, her chin length hair bouncing around her face. Leena sat at a small table we had scrounged up a few weeks back.

Looking between the two of them, I couldn't believe how much they'd changed, Leena especially. If someone told me a year ago, hell even a month ago, that Leena would be laughing and joking with friends, I wouldn't believe them. I would have sooner believed that an alien spaceship would fall through the sky bringing with it, species both fascinating and terrible.

As the universe would have it, both happened.

I didn't know Jeneva very well, but she was so different from the bristly, reclusive person I'd met in the forest when everything first changed. That person, though she did save my life, wanted nothing to do with anyone. Now, Jeneva sought out company whenever she could. She laughed often and loudly and never ran out of things to say.

It was her sister, Amira, who was now the bristly, reclusive one. Part of the reason why we were hanging in a spot in the refugee section of the *Vengeance* was so Jeneva could spend time with Amira. The ship that felt more like home every day, but Amira refused to leave the refugee wing whenever she could help it.

I didn't know the whole story between the two of them, but now that I'd reconciled with Leena, I deeply regretted the time we spent apart, especially after we lost our mother. I would tell Amira as much, she was still a bit prickly. She'd figure it out on her own.

Another woman, Vidia, occasionally joined our little

group. The former mayor of a town that had been destroyed by the Xathi. she had become the de facto leader of the refugees. I had never been to the town, but I heard it had been beautiful. Vidia and roughly a hundred others were the only survivors of that bustling town.

One of those survivors was a little girl, Calixta, Leena's little shadow now. A little bit less so now that'd she'd found a friend to play with, but we all loved having her around.

"What do you think about human men, Mariella?" Jeneva asked me, drawing me back to the here and now.

"All the boys used to love Mariella," Leena answered for me with a knowing smile. "But my sweet sister never gave them the time of day. She was always happier in the library anyway."

I blushed and looked at my hands. It was true, I often turned down dates growing up and in school. The truth was, I never found any of them even remotely interesting. I couldn't be more specific if I tried. They were all just missing...*something.*

"Now she only has eyes for Tu'ver," Leena teased. I could hear a note of unease in her voice, though she was trying to hide it.

I ignored it, tucking a strand of hair behind my ear.

"She's not even trying to deny it," Jeneva chimed in, her tone much warmer than my sisters.

"He's my friend," I said unconvincingly. It was the truth. He was a K'ver and not much of a talker, but I preferred his company to almost anyone else. Though I'd been barely conscious at the time, I still remembered how he carried me out of the dank cave deep in the forest after a spider-like aramirion nearly gutted me.

Tu'ver visited me in the med bay almost every day after that. He was the one who had fitted me with the transmitting device I still wore in my ear, though it was no longer necessary for us to understand each other.

If I was ever able to get back to my own work, the device would be invaluable. Because of it, I could now speak Tu'ver's language, albeit clumsily. He could speak mine as well. When we spoke, we drifted between one language and the other almost without realizing.

I was comfortable with him in a way I didn't feel with anyone else, not even Leena.

Leena scowled, then had the decency to look embarrassed. "Sorry, Mari. There's just something about him that makes me worry about you spending too much time with him."

"He's not the friendliest," Jeneva agreed.

"He saved all of our lives," I argued.

"That's true and we're grateful for that," Leena placated me. "But even Axtin knows to give Tu'ver a wide berth - and that's saying something."

"I think it's sweet that you like him," Jeneva smiled.

"He sure seems to like you. You're the only one he tolerates for an extended period."

I didn't want to admit to either of them how much that idea appealed to me.

"Can we talk about something else?" I asked, twirling a lock of my dark waves between my fingers.

"Leena said something about you spending time in libraries. Is that what you were before all of this happened? A librarian?" Jeneva asked, looking around the refugee bay.

"An archivist," I corrected with a smile. It was a common mistake many made. I never took it personally. Jeneva's brow furrowed in confusion, another common reaction.

I launched into my well-rehearsed explanation. "Most of my work is translating. There were many languages on old Earth. Some of our most important works are in another language entirely. I also track down original paper documents that have yet to be converted to digital."

"I can't remember the last time I saw something written on paper," Jeneva mused.

"Many of the original field surveys from the time of settlement were completed during a period when the electronic systems were still unstable," I answered. "Not all of the details were transcribed into digital later."

There were a few museums in the larger cities. They

were the only places members of the public could view relics like paper documents. I had access to most of the private collections on this world. My favorite was an old library containing nearly a hundred full paper books. I'd been working on transcribing one of them to digital form when my sister showed up at my door.

If she hadn't dragged me into the middle of the jungle that day, we would have never met Jeneva. We probably would have died that day.

"How did you fall into that?" Jeneva asked, tilting her head. I admired her natural curiosity, especially after she spent so long repressing it.

"Originally it was to complement Leena's work," I replied. In the corner of my eye, I saw Leena go a stiff in the shoulders. I was coming too close to talking about our shared secret.

The illness that killed our mother.

Personally, I didn't mind talking about it. I didn't go out of my way to tell people but if someone asked me a direct question I wouldn't lie.

Leena hated the idea of anyone knowing about it. She didn't want to be pitied. Besides me, the only person on the ship who knew about the illness was Axtin, the Valorni male that adored my sister.

"How so?" Jeneva pressed, oblivious to Leena's growing unease.

"Leena and I share many interests, if you can believe

it," I answered, choosing my words carefully. "Our research was similar, though our fields were different. She covered the biological and chemical aspect. I searched for answers through our history. We figured we increased our chances of uncovering something remarkable if we worked together." There was a gleam of excitement in Jeneva's eyes.

"Were you close? What were you looking for?" She asked.

"Mariella," Leena said through clenched teeth.

Jeneva looked to Leena, then back to me.

"Leena, I think we should just tell her," I said with a sigh. "She's a friend. What do you think is going to happen if she knows?" Leena chewed on her bottom lip as she thought it over. Eventually, she sighed, dropping her shoulders and giving me a nod of approval.

"Leena and I have a rare genetic illness," I said, turning my attention back to Jeneva.

Her jaw dropped, and her eyes filled with genuine sadness for us. "That must be awful," she said. "Is it..." She let her voice trail off, but I knew what she meant to ask.

"Yes, it's fatal," I explained. "Leena and I have spent most of our adult lives trying to cure it. More so Leena, that me," I admitted. There was a time where I wanted nothing to do with finding a cure. It was too hard to hope for something that might never happen.

"I'm so sorry," Jeneva said, her voice barely more than a whisper. This was the pity Leena hated. She didn't like to feel weak. I didn't like seeing Jeneva like this because I didn't like the idea of needlessly causing another person to worry. It wasn't Jeneva's fault that I had this illness and it wasn't on her to cure it. She shouldn't have to worry on our behalf. Leena and I worried plenty.

"But we've made a breakthrough recently," Leena cut in. "There's something on this world called N.O.X. I'm not sure what it is exactly, but I accidentally found someone's medical record who came in contact with N.O.X. They showcased many of the same symptoms as the later stages of our illness."

"That's amazing!" Jeneva's face lit up. "So, you think you can cure it?"

"If the universe wants it," I said with a smile and shrug. It was a motto, of sorts. Losing my mother and discovering the illness that lived within me made me feel scared and out of control for a long time.

I had to teach myself that the only way to move past that fear was to give up control. It was easier than I thought it would be. Once I considered how vast the universe was and how small I was in comparison, I found it easier to simply *be*.

When I was still in school, I came across the works of an author who lived on Earth long before my time, long before planetary colonization was even close to possible. His name was Arthur C. Clarke and, centuries ago, he spoke the words that I carry with me now, always.

Magic is just science we don't understand yet.

I believe in that magic.

"I should go," Leena said, bringing me out of my thoughts. "I told Axtin I would have dinner with him tonight, but I have to get some work done at the lab if I'm going to make that happen." She gave me a squeeze on the shoulder before leaving the refugee bay.

"I should get back to work as well," Jeneva said apologetically. She'd been keeping busy recording information about useful properties of the local plants.

I felt useless. Everyone else had an important job to do on the *Vengeance*. I was mostly left to my own devices.

At least all that free time enabled me to make plenty of friends. I knew most of the refugees by name. Same with the *Vengeance* crew.

I preferred talking with the various species found in the crew. Their worlds were fascinating. I could scarcely wrap my head around the fact that they came from a corner of the galaxy that we had no idea existed until the rift tore through everything that separated us.

I got to my feet as Jeneva left, planning on seeking out Tu'ver. It was late enough in the day that he'd probably be done with his shift. Hopefully, he was in the mood for some company. Though even if he wasn't, he wouldn't tell me.

"Wait." A thin hand grabbed my arm as I made my way toward the exit. I stopped, though the hand that grabbed me didn't have the force behind it to stop even a child. The woman who grabbed removed her hand, clutching it to her chest.

Her face was familiar, as all the human faces were now, but I had never spoken to her. She was quiet and kept to herself for the most part. She was thinner than she should be. There was plenty of food to go around now that the food replicators were powered back up.

"Is everything okay?" I asked gently when she didn't say anything more.

"You and your sister," she said, her voice halting and stuttering. "You say you're sick?"

"Yes," I answered honestly. "But it's a genetic illness. It's not contagious," I explained quickly. I could understand why the thought of an illness breaking out in the refugee bay would cause alarm.

"I know," the woman said.

I blinked in surprise. "I've always been a good listener."

"What do you mean?" I asked.

"I'm old and frail," the woman continued without shame. "Most people usually ignore me or don't even notice. So, I listen to the conversations of others to keep me company."

I nodded. She must have overheard everything.

"I heard you two with your friend," she said to me, confirming my own thoughts. "You're sick and you don't know why."

I nodded my head slowly.

"It's not contagious," I repeated, trying to allay her fears.

"And no one knows anything of your illness," she continued, ignoring me.

She was right.

After all this time, Leena and I had never managed to find a documented case of the illness. The woman stared at me, her eyes slightly glassy. I could tell she had been through horrific things before she found her way to the *Vengeance*.

"But," she continued, now looking at me intently. "I might know something about it."

TU'VER

As the doors to my quarters opened, I realized how happy I was that my shift was over. When we aren't out in the world, my job on the ship is to maintain the ship's defensive systems.

I enjoyed my work...manipulating electronics to create more proficient ways to kill came easily to me.

But my conversation with Axtin and Vrehx put me in a sour mood, and having to constantly find parts, or wires, or circuits, or micro-chips to make sure the defensive systems stayed working without proper manufacturing facilities was becoming monotonous and annoying.

As much as I enjoyed my solitude, the task was occasionally wearing.

My room was simple, a bunk on the far wall, a desk

near the door, and a makeshift kitchen that I made for myself out of spare parts, wood from the trees we knocked down when we crashed, and a pair of heating coils from some broken Scrappers. We used the hovercrafts planetside, and I constantly needed to repair them.

I looked in my cooling unit, pondering what I was in the mood for. I pulled out some meat, some vegetables, and the spices I needed and began to cook.

Yes, there was a mess hall and food replicators, but cooking in my quarters had always been a task that allowed me a chance to focus my thoughts.

This had been true for my entire life. On the *Vengeance*, I had set up an informal system with the galley master. I upgraded his equipment from time to time and he passed me over a small amount of the meat that he used for meals that would have been used for my portion anyway.

Meat took a substantial amount of energy to replicate so it seemed like a fair exchange for my services. I also procured certain vegetables from the hydroponics lab and lately, Jeneva had introduced me to local vegetables that wouldn't try to eat me - as certain plants on this planet did - as well.

I remembered back to my first two years in the service. They were terrible. I was reassigned six times, each time in a different corner of the world, and each time with a commanding officer that was fundamentally different than the one before. At times, cooking my own meals had helped me get through the drudgery.

Being moved from assignment to assignment didn't lend itself to creating lasting friendships. I was always reserved around others, more so than even most other K'veri. Most of my time when not carrying out my duties was spent in solitude. I preferred it that way.

Those around me knew to give me a wide berth. There were always rumors about the extent of the training that the military had subjected me to.

If they only knew.

If anything, their conceptions only scratched the surface.

My training had been exhaustive. It had been brutal. And it had been effective.

Even on the *Vengeance*, I knew that regardless of what I was doing, I stood a greater chance to kill another living being than almost anyone on this ship. I didn't have the outward swagger of Axtin or the sense of danger that Vrehx embodied, but my cool, rational nature allowed me to pinpoint an enemy's weakness and exploit it in the shortest amount of time.

I had seen so much killing even in my live training exercises that solitude became preferable to anything else.

Until now.

Now...it almost seemed that Mariella was able to reach through the self-imposed exile I had sent myself into and speak directly to me.

Humans were fragile compared to K'veri. Mariella was more so. But that only seemed to whet the appetite that she brought out in me.

I had served aboard this ship through multiple engagements. I had seen countless battles.

But now I had encountered an enemy towards my solitude that my training had not prepared me for.

My mind was in a tumult. Years of routine created through rational self-exploration were now being turned on their head.

I needed to resolve this. Soon.

I finished cooking my meat and mixed in my vegetables. If it hadn't been for Jeneva, I never would have tried carrot and never would have known that the mickelania root was as tasty as it was. It looked horrible, like something from a creature's bowels, but it tasted fantastic. It was a bit tart, but if cooked in Tilemmin broth, the tartness was tempered and became mouthwatering.

My sister had taught me how to use Tilemmin broth to cook our vegetables. Thinking of her brought a sad smile to face, and I promptly burned my finger. The sudden pain snapped me back to reality.

I bandaged myself and looked at my meal. Without realizing it, I had made Cannira's favorite meal. She always ate Tilemmin stew when she had big news.

She was a lot like Mariella, maybe that was why I liked Mariella so much.

But Cannira was no longer alive. I had failed to save her.

And that's when I realized why I had been silent around Mariella for so long. Why my attraction had been something to suppress rather than inflame.

I feared that in the moment, I would be unable to save Mariella too if she were to get too close.

Perhaps it was time to change that type of thinking and take a gamble.

MARIELLA

I burst through the doors of Leena's lab, nearly causing her to drop the delicate vial of clear liquid she was squinting over.

"Leena!" I rasped, out of breath from running through the ship as fast as I could.

"Stay right there, Mari!" Leena admonished me as the liquid sloshed around in the vial she was operating with some forceps.

"What is that?" I asked, my nose wrinkling at the smell.

"A little present I've been working on for the Xathi," Leena replied, her eyes gleaming with a mixture of pride and spite.

"Does it work?" I asked.

"See for yourself," she said, and poured a bit of the

liquid in the vial into a metal dish that contained some crystals.

I watched in wondering horror as whatever was in that vial ate away at the crystals until they were nothing more than a puddle of sludge.

"I don't know if it will work as effectively yet," she replied with a shrug. "I don't have any Xathi to test it on."

"I'd like to keep it that way, so don't even think about it," I muttered. I could already tell Leena was contemplating finding a way to get a live specimen for testing.

"It would be so much fun, though!" She grinned, a wild look in her eyes. "Just think of it. I could torment them the same way..."

"Leena," I said, my tone softening. My sister went through hell not too long ago. I was amazed that she was able to function as well as she was. If it had been me, I would still be holed up in my room too scared to ever step out again.

But, then again, Leena had always been the stronger sister. I wasn't totally helpless, but I definitely did not have her iron will.

"I'm fine," Leena said firmly. She used to snarl when anyone asked. I considered this progress. "What made you come running in here like a mad thing anyway?"

"There's a woman in the refugee bay who says she

might know something about the genetic illness," I explained quickly.

Leena gave me an exasperated look.

"Mariella, are you going to tell everyone about it? Because if you are, we should just make a ship wide broadcast announcement. It would save us the time," she sighed.

"I didn't tell her anything," I said in defense. "She overhead us talking about it with Jeneva."

"Well, what did she say?" Leena asked.

"I asked her to wait," I replied. "I wanted to come find you first. Hurry up, she's waiting."

Leena nodded and quickly cleaned up the lab area. We walked briskly through the labyrinth of hallways that were now as familiar to me as my hometown until we were back in the refugee bay.

"Leena, this is Sidra," I said, gesturing to the woman. She looked uneasy. Her thin arms were wrapped around her small body. Her eyes darted around the space behind us like she was waiting for something to jump from the shadowy places of the room.

"Nice to meet you," Leena said in a low, gentle voice that I hadn't heard her use before she was held captive on a Xathi ship.

I was glad something awakened my sister's compassionate side, but I would've given anything for it to have been done differently.

"My name is Leena," my sister continued. She extended her hand for Sidra to shake. Sidra just stared at it. After a moment, Leena retracted her hand. "My sister tells me you might know something about a genetic illness."

Sidra gave a jerky nod.

"My father's aunt died young," Sidra explained. She swayed slightly as she spoke, slowly shifting her weight from foot to foot. "She was always sick, even though she'd been perfectly healthy before. One by one her organs started to fail. Even at an early age she would get tired easily. She was forty-eight when she died."

"I'm very sorry to hear that," Leena said, gently placing a hand on Sidra's shoulder. Sidra filched at the touch but relaxed when it became clear Leena wasn't going to do anything more than that. "Our mother died the same way."

"My grandfather died shortly after my father's aunt," Sidra continued. "He was fifty-two. He died the exact same way." She was remarkably calm while explaining the deaths in her family. With a sinking heart, I realized she must have been through things far worse.

"What about your grandfather's parents?" Leena pressed.

"They both lived into their eighties," Sidra shrugged. "My father is going to be sixty-three this year if he…"

she trailed off but Leena and I both knew what she meant. If he was still alive.

I was struck by the bittersweet realization that Leena and I were lucky, in an odd way. Our mother was dead, and we hadn't seen our father since we were small children. We were each other's only family and we were fortunate to be together now.

"Did your aunt have any children before she passed?" Leena asked.

Genetics wasn't my field of expertise, but even I knew it was strange that Sidra's grandfather had a similar condition to our mother but didn't pass it on to Sidra's father.

"No, she never married or had kids," Sidra replied. There was more clarity in her eyes now and she was no longer swaying. She looked more comfortable with us that she did when she first approached me.

Perhaps speaking with people and having normal conversations had somewhat helped her. I promised myself I would make more time in my day to talk to her.

Leena's brow was furrowed, her mouth was pinched. I could practically see the wheels spinning in her head as she tried to make sense of everything.

"Where did your grandfather and great-aunt live?" She asked.

"Glymna," Sidra answered. "They were both part of

the first survey team. I guess you could say they were some of the founding members of the town." The hint of pride in her voice was unmistakable.

Leena looked at Sidra for long moments. eyes sparkling. I hoped that she had been given something useful.

"Thank you so much for sharing that with us," Leena finally said, a bit quickly before continuing. "Mari, let's go."

Leena grabbed my hand and dragged me back to the lab before I could even say goodbye to Sidra. She looked confused, and a little sad, as Leena and I bolted away.

"That was rude!" I admonished as Leena pulled me back through the hallways. Some of the crew gave us strange, but amused looks, as we hurried past.

I smiled at everyone I recognized. They were likely used to me and my sister roaming around and acting strange.

"I'll apologize later," Leena said over her shoulder. Once we were back in the lab with the door shut, Leena took me by my shoulders.

"I already know what you're going to say, and I don't think it justifies the dramatic exit you just made," I sighed, holding back a laugh. Leena always had a flair for the dramatic, though I don't think she was fully aware of it.

"What am I going to say, then? Since you know everything," she said, placing her hands on her hips.

"Our grandmother was on the same survey team," I supplemented.

"And she showed signs of the same illness that took mom," Leena finished. "I think that the genetic condition can only be passed from mothers to their children and it started with that survey team. Why don't you seem excited about this?"

"I am!" I said quickly. "I'm just trying not to laugh at you."

"What's so funny?" Leena demanded, her eyes narrowing. "This is my life's work, Mari. It explains why you sometimes get tired and sleep for days. It explains why Mom died so young. I *finally* have something to go on and you think it's a joke."

"I don't think it's a joke, Leena," I said, keeping my voice even and calm as hers started to pitch. "It's my life on the line too. It's my life's work too."

"Work you gave up for years," Leena shot back.

"Yes," I sighed. "I gave it up because I needed to teach myself how to live a good life in case we never found a cure."

"You gave up," Leena repeated coldly.

"This, what we're doing right now, is exactly why I stopped working for a while," I said. "As our research picked up, you became less like a sister and more like a colleague. An unpleasant one, at that."

"I'm not going to apologize for being dedicated to my work," Leena said, lifting her chin defiantly.

"I'm not asking you to," I replied. "And I know it's hard for you to understand this, but I would've rather had a strong relationship with my sister and a shorter but happy life, then spend every waking moment terrified of all my work meaning nothing in the end."

"You're right, I don't understand that at all," Leena huffed.

"Have you ever just been content?" I asked. "Have you ever stopped at any point in your life and been happy with exactly where you were?"

My question threw her off, I could tell.

"What does that matter?" She said after a few moments. "I'll be happy and content once we find a cure."

"That makes me incredibly sad for you, Leena," I said hoping she could tell I was being genuine. "You've made so much progress since we ended up on this ship."

"What's that supposed to mean?" Leena snapped.

"You and I have spoken more in the past few weeks than we have in the past few years," I continued. "We talk. We joke. We have friends. You found someone who would walk through fire for you. Literally. Don't go back to using your work as an excuse to keep everyone at arm's length. We deserve better. And, more importantly, you deserve better."

"At least I don't put every bit of my energy into keeping my head shoved firmly up my ass so I can pretend I'm an ethereal force of goodness that's *so content* with life even though it's gone to shit," she sneered. "Pull yourself out of the fantasy world you live in and grow up, Mari."

That stung.

Yes, I did put nearly all my energy into trying to find something to be happy about even in the darkest of circumstances. I couldn't understand why Leena thought that was a bad thing.

However, this was a conversation I no longer wished to be a part of. I'd bruised Leena's pride. She would only get meaner if I kept pushing her. She needed time to step away and think.

And, honestly, so did I.

"I'm going to try to get on my old work network. Maybe I'll be able to find something on the first Glymna survey," I said, keeping my head up.

I knew Leena didn't mean what she said. She only lashed out because she knew what I said was true and she wasn't ready to accept it. She would come around. I would probably find a datapad with a hastily scrawled apology stuck to my door in the morning.

But as I made my way back to my room, a part of me wondered if Leena had a point.

There was only one person I could think of talking to at this point.

But I didn't know if he even wanted to be bothered with this. I'd have to decide soon.

Perhaps I needed to roll the dice and find out.

I'd seen him countless times, but somehow for this meeting with Tu'ver I hesitated.

Before I saw him, I needed something more appealing to wear.

TU'VER

I needed to see Mariella.

It was becoming unbearable to be away from her.

Her differences from the other two women were more than just her physical appearance, it was her demeanor and attitude towards everyone that set her apart. She was shorter than Jeneva by several inches, and only a bit taller than Leena, and I loved her compact size...it fit me better.

Her dark hair, her darker skin, and her slim form kept me awake at night, and when I did sleep, my dreams—the ones that I remembered—were filled with her.

But it was how she acted that attracted me most.

She was quiet, gentle, and more willing than the other humans to give us a chance.

Even though Leena and Jeneva had spent the last couple of months "adventuring" with us and spending their time with Vrehx and Axtin, they still weren't as comfortable around the crew as Mariella was.

Mariella was a natural go-between for the various races aboard the *Vengeance*. She talked with the humans, constantly reassuring them that we were trying to help. She spoke to us as though we had always been part of her life.

But that added to my attraction to Mariella...no matter who she talked to or how they were feeling, she was able to talk to them and rarely let them bother her.

Leena upset her, but that was a sibling thing, something I knew all too well.

There was something I did know about Mariella, she loved to read. She had already read everything in my personal collection, and I knew she was working her way through Captain Rouhr's reading collection as well.

As an archivist, she had taken her love of reading and knowledge and turned it into a career unlike most others, and that made her important to the people of Ankau. It was her job to translate and transpose information from physical copy to digital copy, as well as translate or interpret the older texts into more modern translations.

Then it dawned on me.

There was one thing Mariella did not know.

She did not know how I felt.

I was the hunter. All I had to do was to go catch her.

I headed over to the ship's library. Our library was a small room, with several datapads dedicated to research shelved in the room. There was a central console with several ports extending from it, allowing us to download anything our computer had access to onto a datapad.

I did a quick search, found something I thought would interest her that hadn't been accessed in months, downloaded it to the datapad, and left the library.

I went to her room, excited to see her.

I fully knew how odd this situation was.

I could line up a shot and pull the trigger, putting a round through the brain of an enemy without hesitation.

Talking to any other female, I had no issues.

But with Mariella?

It felt so very different.

My hand hovered in the air near her door for who-knows-how-many seconds before I finally knocked on her door.

Normally when I knocked on her door, it was only a

few short moments before she answered, but this time it took a bit longer for her to get to the door. I heard noises coming from inside, and just as I was about to lean in to hear better, her door opened.

She was a bit wide-eyed when she answered the door, and looked a bit disheveled, almost as if she had been changing clothes hastily and had forgotten to straighten herself up.

It didn't matter. She was gorgeous.

"Hello there, Tu'ver," she said with a genuine smile. "What can I do for you?"

"I brought you a book to read," I said to her, flashing her a smile. "I figured you had already gone through everything else." I cursed my cockiness, but the smile in her eyes made me feel bigger than I was.

"Oh? That's so sweet, thank you. Come in," she said as she stepped aside, letting me into her room. At a quick glance, it was a basic room stretching nearly twenty feet in one direction and thirteen feet in another. The females had been given the dignitary rooms as their quarters, so their rooms were bigger and better furnished than normal guest quarters.

Right now, hers was a bit messy. There were papers, datapads, and notes strewn all over the living area of the room. Her bed was a mess. She had been occupied with something.

"Sorry for the mess, I was a little busy trying to

figure something out," she said, echoing my own thoughts.

I turned to look at her and tried to give her my best smile. "That is understandable then. Is everything all right?"

"Huh? Oh, yeah," she hesitated, then waved off my question. "Just got caught up with some stuff, that's all. So, you said you found a new book for me?"

I nodded as I handed her the pad. "Yes. It took me quite some time to find something for you to read, but I think this might be something that would interest you. It's a story from my homeland."

"Nice." She stroked the datapad, eyes soft. "Thank you. I really appreciate it." Simple words.

But this time, from her they seemed to mean a great deal.

But now...it was time for my surprise.

"I hope you like it. It took me a while to find it in the library database."

Her head snapped up like a spring. Her eyes were wide and the look on her face worried me a bit. It was the look of someone that had found their next hit of something euphoric.

The last time I had seen a face like that, besides when Axtin was able to get into a fight with something, was back home in the slums of Alten Sajohno when several of my childhood classmates searched for their next dose of Voi, a hallucinogenic spice that had been running rampant during my more immature years.

She tried to keep her voice calm, but I could hear the vibrato of excitement in her words. "There's a library on board? Where?"

I felt compelled to answer, as if I was under some sort of spell. "It's...the main access point is a few levels up from here. I can show you, if you want."

She smiled, and jumped to the door, nearly shaking in anticipation as I stepped towards her.

"Are you okay?"

"Hmm? Yeah, just want to see this library of yours. How come you never told me about it? Can I access it from my computer terminal? What kind of stuff is in there?"

I tried to answer her questions, but I'm not sure she heard me. She was in such a rush to get to the library that she practically dragged me to the nearest lift. She squeezed through the doors as they opened, pulling me behind her.

I pushed the button to go up and she was out of the doors before they finished opening again. I tried to slow her down by reminding her she didn't know where it was, and I could see the slight disappointment in her eyes, but she slowed down.

I hated seeing that disappointment, it hurt me to see that look in her eyes. I had to fight my own urge to hurry just to make her feel better, so I slowed down on purpose. She tried to grab me, but I side-stepped and blocked her.

She practically yelled at me, but I kept walking. I asked what she was so excited for, but she blew me off. When I looked back at her, I fought back a smile and mentioned that she was acting a bit twitchy.

She laughed me off, said something about loving to read, and grabbed me by the wrist, trying to pull me faster. Of course, she missed the corridor the library was down, but I didn't say anything…I was enjoying the tease too much.

Finally, I took her down the right corridor and stopped in front of the library, but I hesitated.

"Are you going to tell me what this is all about?" I asked, folding my arms.

She put her hands on her hips, did an over-exaggerated roll of her eyes, and said that she'd tell me. I chuckled to myself and coded the door open for her.

It was a beautiful dance that we did. And I was beginning to think it was one I could do forever.

MARIELLA

I got the distinct feeling that Tu'ver was walking slow on purpose.

I stepped to one side, planning to grab his arm and force him to walk faster but he predicted my movements and blocked me.

"Are you kidding me?" I cried, exasperated but still laughing.

"Tell me what you're after and I'll pick up the pace," Tu'ver said over his shoulder. Once again, I was perplexed by Leena's apparent dislike of Tu'ver.

This is how we always were together. We teased each other. We annoyed each other. More specifically, Tu'ver teased me and I annoyed him.

I knew I was the exception, not the rule. I was aware of the strange looks we got when we walked around the

Vengeance together. People looked at me like I was walking alongside a Kaitrix, or something equally terrifying.

"Why do I have to be after anything?" I said with an innocent shrug. "Can't a girl just read some books?"

Tu'ver turned to look at me as we walked. His expression looked blank, but I'd known him long enough to notice the slight upturn in the corner of his mouth and the faint glimmer of amusement in his black eyes.

"I've never seen you this twitchy and you're trying to tell me you just want to read?" He said, clearly not believing me.

"I'm an archivist who hasn't been in a library in months. Of course, I want to read," I said, grabbing his wrist and pulling him forward. Even though I was throwing my full weight against him, he barely picked up the pace.

I looked back at him. He looked like he was going to burst out laughing. "Having fun back there?" I quipped.

"Immense fun," he chuckled. "You look ridiculous."

"And you look just as ridiculous," I replied.

"I doubt that," he smirked. "And the library is down that corridor back there, by the way."

I stopped short, nearly causing Tu'ver to run into me.

"Are you enjoying this?" I asked, gently pushing him back down the hallway.

"Very much," he replied. I didn't mind that I was the object of his mockery. He was the object of mine just as often.

I liked seeing this side of him. When he was with others, or among the members of his own strike team, he was must more stoic and reserved.

But with me, he laughed and joked and teased like the world wasn't falling apart around us. Without him, without his friendship, I think I would've gone quite mad by now.

He stopped in front of a door identical to the others, but he hesitated before opening it.

"Are you going to tell me what this is all about?" He asked, folding his arms across the broad expanse of his chest.

"If there is anything to tell, I will tell you. Deal?" I sighed, putting my hands on my hips with a dramatic eye roll. He chuckled and shook his head before opening the door.

I don't know what I was expecting. I knew that the ship's library wouldn't be anything like the archives I used to work in. But I was expecting more than what it was.

It was a closet really. Large enough for perhaps four individuals to stand comfortably. The walls were lined with row upon row of thin data disks, each faintly glowing blue to indicate they were empty. At the back of the room were two standing computer consoles and one port for downloading.

"Wow," I said flatly. "It's so…"

"It's not much, I know," Tu'ver shrugged. If I didn't know better, I would think he was a little embarrassed. "We don't have much use for a central library aboard the *Vengeance*." It was darker in this room than it was in the hallway. The low light made the intricate circuitry in Tu'ver's skin appear to glow brighter.

"I think it's cozy," I said with a smile. "All it needs is a comfy chair and it would be perfect."

"You're a bad liar," Tu'ver replied.

"Give me credit for trying," I laughed. I quickly crossed the small room to one of the computers. The holographic screen flickered to life as I approached. I felt a small swell of pride as I was able to understand almost every character of the alien's written language.

"Tu'ver," I asked slowly, turning to him. He stood at attention, his eyes roaming my body. "Is there any way to connect this library to my university work station?"

"That's not how it's programmed," he said to me.

He must have noticed my disappointment. Because he took a step closer.

"Humans   are   too   decentralized   to   connect

everything," he said, closing the distance between us until he was shoulder to shoulder with me in front of the computer. "But let me try something." The circuits on his arms began to glow more intensely. He placed his hand flat against a black panel on the side of the computer. I watched his eyes flicker back and forth under closed lids.

The computer chirped and suddenly thousands of databases were popping up on the screen.

"What did you just do?" I asked in wonder.

"I just linked every database on this planet to the console," he said smoothly. I didn't miss the hint of pride in his voice. "We won't be connected to private repositories but anything that allows public access can be viewed from here."

"Amazing!" I gasped before diving into the virtual sea of information. Tu'ver might have said something to me, but I didn't hear him. I was instantly absorbed into the world of research. Many of the databases weren't useful to me. I sifted through them quickly.

I stepped away from the computer console to grab a handful of empty data disks. I didn't have a proper office like I usually would, but I was determined to make do.

"Watch this," Tu'ver said with a sly smile. He typed in a few commands and the bare wall in front of the computers lit up displaying the research I'd pulled.

"Thank you!" I beamed. I didn't know what I would do without him.

The Glymna survey team seemed like the easiest place to start. It would've been extremely well documented. However, the tricky part was finding information I didn't already know. I quickly eliminated information from the databases that were available to the public. I needed original field notes and personal logs.

I couldn't find information on every single member of the original survey team in Glymna. I did find several pictures of my grandmother with twenty or so others dressed for an expedition. Their skinsuits would've been standard at the time, as were the blasters. There was a man standing in the row behind my grandmother that looked strikingly similar to Sidra. Her grandfather, I presumed.

"Can I see medical records now?" I asked Tu'ver. He was watching me intently. "You don't have to stay if you have something better to do," I said quickly. I didn't mind having him here. I preferred his presence to solitude. But I couldn't imagine this was entertaining for him.

"It's interesting to watch you work," he replied. "And yes. You should be able to view medical records."

"Oh, well I wouldn't say I'm working," I said

hesitantly. It was the truth. This sort of thing was not usually what I did. This was for Leena.

"Whatever you say," Tu'ver said with a lazy smile. He picked out a blank data disk before walking over to the second computer console beside me. Another day, I would've been curious about what he chose to read.

I liked almost everything he brought me from his personal collection. I probably would've liked what he picked out now. But figuring this out, finding something to make Leena happy, was more important now. Of course, I was invested in this research for my own obvious reasons but right now I felt that it was more important that Leena knew she wasn't in this alone.

I found the medical records for as many of the original survey team members as I could.

So much for patient confidentiality, I thought wryly. But my brief flash of humor quickly fizzled away when I examined the team's medical records.

They were all dead, which wasn't too surprising.

But, nearly all of them had died in the same way.

The same way my mother died.

The same way Leena and I were going to die if we didn't figure this out.

The thought should have scared me more, but it didn't. I was looking at a list of symptoms and facts. Nothing more.

I was certain that the survey team encountered whatever caused the genetic illness. But it couldn't possibly be where people lived currently. I broadened my search to include all Glymna's residents since its founding. When I compared the postmortem reports of everyone that had any symptoms resembling the illness, a clear pattern emerged.

Leena's theory was right. It was likely most, or all the team was exposed to something that caused the illness, maybe the mysterious N.O.X, maybe something else, but only the children of the women had inherited the condition.

I was glad that it affected so few people, relatively speaking that is. But it made gathering data more difficult.

From what the records told me, anyone in Glymna who could have carried the genetic condition had already passed away. None of the women bore any children. Perhaps they knew what they would pass on to them. I wondered if my mother knew, would she still have had us?

I made more notes on my data pad and transferred a few more files I thought would be useful. I now had a collection of documents that would rival any of my files back home.

There was still a gigantic piece of the puzzle missing and I was pretty damn sure I would find it in Glymna.

After all there were probably records that weren't open to the public interfaces and needed to be accessed in person. There may even be paper based records that had the necessary information but were never digitized because on one ever knew their importance.

I just needed to find a way to get there. I slowly turned to face Tu'ver, who was leaning up against one of the walls scrolling through his own data pad.

"It must have been interesting," he said simply.

"Why?" I asked back."

"Do you know how long we've been here?" he asked without raising his head.

"I have to ask you something," I said, my voice quiet.

"You've been staring at the console for almost four hours," he said. "I think you went a full hour without blinking once."

When I didn't respond with something quippy and clever, he looked up at me. "Mariella, what is it?" he asked, tilting his head slightly to one side. His expression became one of concern.

"I need your help," I said, the desperation finally breaking through my voice. "It's a matter of life and death."

"Mine."

TU'VER

Mariella, my sweet, calm Mariella, had gone
insane.

That was the only thing that could explain her
request.

"I need to go to Glymna!" she said with such
insistence that she practically bounced. "Don't you get
it? There's information there that could help Leena and
me with our research!"

"What research are the two of you doing that it's
important enough to go through Xathi territory to
get it?"

The hesitation on her face told me enough.

She didn't want to tell me, but I wasn't going to let
her go without knowing what this was all about.

"It doesn't matter, we just have to get there. It's important."

"Well," I said slowly. "If it's so important, then you won't mind telling me what it is exactly, so I know what we're doing."

There had to be a reason she was so headstrong about going to Glymna and there was no way a few simple papers were enough.

She looked at me, biting her lower lip as she visibly fought with herself over whether or not to tell me. "Can't you just trust me?"

"I do trust you," I responded back to her. "But I can't let you go there just for some documents. Rouhr wouldn't allow it and I can't let you go. It's too dangerous."

"Please!" She looked at me with such pain that my chest ached, but I had to stay firm. "I don't want to see that look on your face that everyone has."

"What look?"

"Pity. Sorrow. Please don't make me tell you."

"Think about what you just said," I told her as I put my hands on her shoulders. "You don't want me to pity you and feel sorrow for you, but now that's all I'm going to be thinking since you said it." I drew her in and hugged her, holding her close. "Tell me so I don't have to worry if anything is wrong."

I could feel her breathing. I imagined her thinking through whatever it was that was bothering her, debating with herself if she should tell me or not.

Eventually, she pulled away from me, wiped some tears from her eyes, and took a deep, shaky breath.

"My sister and I, and maybe other people on this planet, have a genetic disease." Her voice had calmed. "It'll start messing with my organs and shutting down my immune system. Already I sometimes get very tired. It makes me weak and I usually have to sleep for a while before I'm better. If it works like it did with our grandmother and our mother, we'll both be dead around fifty."

I took a deep breath and stared at her.

"Tu'ver? Are you okay?"

I wasn't sure how she could be so calm about this. Perhaps it's because she knew about it for a long time, perhaps it's because she's better at processing this kind of information, perhaps it's because of who she is...

The idea of an enemy that I couldn't fight scared me beyond reason.

Yet, here she was, outwardly looking and sounding like this was something that was just another part of life.

"Please don't feel bad for us, Tu'ver. We've known about this disease for years, but we have a chance!" Her sudden enthusiasm snapped me out of my thoughts. "Leena found something, something that can help us. And I think the information she needs, that we both need, is in Glymna. That's why I need to go."

"Okay, okay. Lower your voice a little. Let me think about this for a moment."

If I ever hoped to have a long life with this woman, I would have to help her fight something that I couldn't see. Who was I to stop from chasing down hope? Who was I to stop her from trying to live?

What she proposed was a trip through the forest where the Xathi were roaming free, then through the plains where there was absolutely no cover, and finally up into the mountains—and all of this depended on whether Glymna was still free of Xathi influence, how they dealt with seeing me, and whether Rouhr would let us go.

Rouhr would never let us go.

Axtin's shot that broke the sub-queen's head had sent the Xathi into a bit of a rage that hadn't calmed in the two weeks since.

So…we would have to sneak out and do this as just the two of us. No need to get anyone else into trouble over this. This would be my decision, my mission, my violation of the rules.

Well…apparently, I had already decided to take her. The only thing left to do was figure out how.

"Alright, we're going." She started to hop in joy, but I stopped her. "Before you get all excited, this is something that we have to keep quiet. Rouhr won't allow us to go because of the Xathi, so if the others come with, that's too many people gone on something he doesn't know about or approve."

"But we're going?" She struggled to hold her voice down. Her excitement was infectious, and I found myself smiling.

"We just need to get some supplies and one of the Scrappers."

"A what now?"

"A Scrapper," I repeated. "It's one of our hover sleds. Most of them were damaged in the crash and I've been working on trying to fix them, that's why we haven't used any. I've only gotten three of them up and running so far, and I'm not sure about two of them."

"Will the working Scrapper make it there?" she asked. I could see her figuring the distance to Glymna in her head and trying to imagine what the trip would be like.

I tilted my head to the side and thought about it for a second. Then, with a drawn-out breath, I answered her. "Y-y-yes?"

She shot me a look. "'Yes' as a statement or 'yes' as a question?"

That's when I explained to her that the Scrappers

were single-pilot machines. They were strong enough to carry the *weight* of three people, but there wasn't enough *room* for even two people. If we took it, it would be a very tight and uncomfortable fit.

"How long would it take to get us there?" She obviously didn't mind the idea of a tight fit.

"It should be fast enough to get us there in one night, hopefully."

"Then let's do it. What do we need?"

I chuckled and raised my arm pad to make a list of our supplies. I sent her data pad a list of things that she needed to get and needed to bring.

But not before she gave me a hug. After a moment, she released me and stepped back.

"Thank you, Tu'ver," she said looking at me. "For everything."

I nodded, and we parted. She went back to her quarters and I went to the supply room and armory.

I gave myself a chance to wonder just how much power this woman held over me as I prepared for our excursion. It was the height of madness.

But I would do anything to ensure her survival.

By the time I came back to my quarters, I had concluded that while I would accompany Mariella, the first sign of trouble would send us back to the *Vengeance*. If afterwards we needed to take a full-scale raiding party to acquire the information she wanted, so be it.

We would find a way to fix this disease.

And Mariella would be happy and safe.

And mine.

Forever.

MARIELLA

I was already awake when I heard the soft knock at my door. I padded across the room and hoped the door wouldn't be too loud when it slid open.

Tu'ver frowned when he saw me.

"You're going to need something warmer than that," he advised.

"This is the warmest thing I have," I said gesturing to the fitted black pants and the plain black tactical shirt I wore. He frowned a bit and looked like he was going to say something else, but I cut him off. "It'll be fine. Let's just go before someone stops us."

We walked slowly through the passageways leading to the docking bay. The plan was to look as casual as possible. If anyone stopped us, which wasn't likely, I would say I was having trouble sleeping and Tu'ver was keeping me company. Everyone knew we were close. It wouldn't raise any suspicions. And there weren't many people on board who'd question Tu'ver.

The *Vengeance* was darker at this time of night. Most of the main overhead lights were turned off. Only the patchy floor lights lining the walkways and the lights that illuminated the computer stations were left on. Darkness always made me feel a little uncomfortable.

I linked my arm through Tu'ver's as we walked. As if he could sense my nervousness, he placed his hand over mine.

No one on night duty acknowledged us as we walked. The closer we got to the docking bay, the more I was able to relax. Earlier this evening, I left a note for Leena in her lab. If Tu'ver and I weren't back in two days, Leena would get help.

As far as any of us knew, the Xathi had yet to show any interest in Glymna. It was the farthest city from the capital, Nyhiem. It was unlikely that we would run into any once we crossed the occupied areas.

Tu'ver strode through the doors of the docking bay, nodding at the Skotan that was standing guard. The Skotan nodded back but said nothing. I looked up at Tu'ver, my disbelief written all over my face.

"Confidence is key," he whispered with a wink.

I rolled my eyes.

"Well, you weren't confident that one of

these...Scrappers could get to Glymna and yet here we are," I whispered back.

"You were the one practically on your knees begging me to help you," he reminded me with a sly grin. "Besides, I worked on these myself. Don't you trust me?"

"I do," I sighed. "Thank you for helping me. It means the world to Leena and me." He opened his mouth to say something, a snarky remark most likely. But instead he simply lowered his head.

"You're welcome," he said. He stepped away from me to boot up the Scrapper. Cold air rushed into the space where he'd been. I shivered.

The Scrappers were clearly meant to hold a single passenger. The streamlined body was hollowed out to make room for a compact, but complex, control panel and a single deep seat for the pilot. Its wings were short and about half as long as the body was. A flying silver bullet.

"Keep watch while I make some adjustments," he said, bending over the control panel of the Scrapper. I turned and faced the door, where the Skotan guard was waiting on the other side. Despite my fear of being caught, I couldn't help but steal glances at Tu'ver as he worked.

The circuits on his arms lit up like they did in the library. The lights on the Scrappers control panel flickered and blinked. It was like they were having a conversation.

"What are you doing?" I whispered, letting my curiosity get the better of me.

"When we take the Scrapper out of its dock, a notification will appear in the command center of the *Vengeance*. I'm making sure that won't happen," he explained. "I'm also going to disable the automatic tracker."

"Do you think that's a good idea?" I asked. "What if something happens and we need rescue?"

"I can turn it back on with as little as a thought." He smiled in reassurance. "And I've brought my nav unit. I can update our location whenever we think there might be trouble. And we aren't completely defenseless either." Tu'ver nodded to the small gear bag that contained a blaster for each of us and a few compact grenades in addition to the food and water I tucked away.

"Okay," I said, still feeling uneasy. Maybe this wasn't such a good plan.

"I've amplified the stealth system as well," Tu'ver continued. "If anything is scanning for us, we won't show up on the radar. If no one notices the Scrapper is missing, we can make it to Glymna and back before anyone knows we're gone."

"And how likely is it that no one will notice we're

missing?" I asked.

"Incredibly unlikely. They will probably realize we're gone before sunup," he said bluntly.

I stared at him, open-mouthed. He shrugged. "I was attempting to put your mind at ease. It's not my fault you ask so many questions."

"You're ridiculous," I snorted.

"Would you like me to lie to you next time?" He asked. I couldn't tell if he was joking or not.

"No, I always appreciate your honesty," I answered truthfully. "Humans lie a lot. And most of them are good at it. It's nice to know I don't have to worry about that with you."

"Glad I can be of service," he said before returning his attention to the Scrapper control panel. After a few more minutes, he straightened back up. "We should be good to go now."

"Okay," I said, stepping closer to the Scrapper. I surveyed the cramped pilot compartment. "How do you want to do this?"

"I'll get in first," he said. "And then you can just..."

"Squeeze myself in?" I finished with a profound eyeroll. "Fun."

"If I move the seat as far back as possible, you should be able to fit between myself and the control panel," Tu'ver suggested. He moved the seat back and climbed in before lifting his arms up, so I could sort myself out.

"I'm going to try really hard not to step on you," I said as I stepped into the cockpit.

"You're doing a terrible job," Tu'ver winced.

"Sorry!" I said quickly shifting my weight. I lost my balance and tumbled into the space between Tu'ver and the control console.

"That's one way to do that," he groaned. "Are you all right?"

"I've been better," I grumbled. "After this, no more secret research trips."

"Agreed. Are you comfortable?" He asked, trying to find the best place to put his arms.

"No," I said. I couldn't help but laugh at the situation. We must look ridiculous. "Are you?"

"Not in the slightest," he replied, a smirk pulling at the corner of his mouth. "You aren't in crippling pain though, right?"

"No," I said. "And you're not being crushed under the weight of me?"

"I've had Axtin sit on me. Believe me, you're no trouble," he said.

"That's a story I've got to hear," I insisted. Tu'ver powered up the Scrapper. It hummed quietly as Tu'ver slowly backed it out of its port.

"It's not as funny as it sounds," he warned.

"Tell me anyway," I replied. "We've got a lot of time to kill."

"It was a few weeks back on a scouting mission," Tu'ver started. "The whole strike team had to squeeze into a transport unit that was meant for three people, four at the most. Axtin was running late. We had already figured out where everyone was going to sit but he decided to climb on top of us, so he wouldn't get left behind."

"That sounds about right," I chuckled. I liked Axtin. He was always good for a laugh, but he never thought anything through. Leena said he gave her headaches, but I think she liked his unpredictability. It was good for her.

"Joke was on him. Every time the transport unit shifted it drove my knee into an unfavorable part of his body," Tu'ver chuckled.

"I doubt he learned anything from that experience," I giggled.

"Probably not," Tu'ver agreed. We rode in comfortable silence for a little over an hour before I started to feel tired. I should have tried to sleep more once we solidified our plan. But I was just too nervous. I'd never done anything like this before.

My eyelids felt heavy and my legs ached. I shifted, trying my best not to bump Tu'ver, until my back was against the bottom of the console and my head rested on Tu'ver's shoulder.

Nothing protected us from the bitter bite of the night air from invading the Scrapper. I burrowed closer to Tu'ver to escape it. Absentmindedly, I ran a finger along the faintly glowing circuitry on his arm. It felt no different from his normal skin, which looked almost pitch black in the low light instead of the usual steel gray.

I stifled a yawn, fighting to stay awake.

"Sleep if you need to," Tu'ver said gently.

"No, I'm fine," I mumbled but my eyes were already closing.

In the last few moments before I lost consciousness, all I was aware of was how warm and solid Tu'ver felt. I was overcome with the same feeling I felt when he carried me out of the cave. Even before I knew him, before we could understand each other's languages, I felt safe with him then. And I felt safe with him now.

He'd saved my life once. He risked his life to save Leena, too. Now he risked everything again to take me to Glymna. I only hoped that one day I would be able to return his kindness.

TU'VER

The pre-dawn light gave me my first close look at the mountains. Even the smallest peak rose thousands of feet above me, and we were still several miles away.

Mariella nodded off beneath me, as I maneuvered the Scrapper around a tree stump. Only a few trees dotted the plains, I had counted five since leaving the forest, including the stump. Just off to my left, towards the south, a broad river crossed the landscape.

Just inside the borders of the mountains would be a bridge if the accounts were right. These mountains intrigued me.

The mountains of my home were small and worn down. These were tall, jagged, and seemed to challenge the sky for supremacy. Another few minutes brought us into the outer parts of the mountain range. The sides of the mountain towered over us, the sheer cliffs stretching above us like giants.

The trail was clean, as were the walls of the mountain for the first twenty feet, as if the trail was cut into the mountain. The trail had two bends before the cliff faces stopped, and there was the bridge we had to cross to get to Glymna.

I stopped the Scrapper to look. A suspension bridge, twenty-feet wide and almost three hundred feet long, while the river roared a hundred feet below, the white caps visible as they raced down the way.

A bird screeched above us, answered by a similar screech from one of the cliffs behind us. A quick glance up let me see something with four wings fly into a small outcropping in the cliff face, greeted by the sounds of several little chitters and screeches. Smiling, I turned back to the bridge.

It looked in good shape, nothing seemed out of order. The tension cables looked strong, their anchors seemed to be correctly in place, and everything seemed in order.

Yet, I hesitated.

Part of my mind laughed at me, a sniper, a warrior that used heights to his advantage to get the shot, was hesitating about going over a bridge.

It wasn't the height, I rationalized to myself.

It was the fact that I was on a single occupant hover sled, carrying a woman who had changed my outlook on life.

Risks that I would have gladly taken before became difficult to fathom with this woman involved.

We were headed to a place that may or may not have answers to questions she had. And even though the bridge was twenty feet across, if she moved too much or a strong gust of wind hit us too hard, there would be nothing to stop us from falling.

I looked down at Mariella. She slept too deeply for it to be sheer exhaustion. The disease she spoke of had probably made her weak and she would probably not be able to wake for a while.

Borrowing the Scrapper, the trip through the forest and around Xathi patrols, and finally the long run through the plains had worn her out, not to mention whatever else she had done before I brought her the data disk that started this little adventure. All of this was happening because of something that was killing her.

Would kill her.

I couldn't let that happen.

And so, my decision was made simple.

I took us across the bridge. Despite my worries, the crossing was smooth and straightforward.

The trail continued off to the right, its passage back

into the mountains blocked by some boulders. I took us carefully around the boulders and into the mountains. They blocked the light of the rising sun, making it difficult to see without the Scrapper's lights.

After about fifteen minutes of travel, we came to a dead end. Somehow, I must have missed a turn somewhere. Doubling back, I found the trail that was cut into the mountain...a tunnel cut through the face of the mountain. It was too small for the Scrapper. We would have to walk. I looked down at her unconscious form.

I would have to walk.

I stopped the Scrapper and gently laid her down against it. I reorganized our supplies, put both packs on my back, then picked her up. The tunnel was big enough to walk through it comfortably, if you were okay with tight spaces.

I had lost all light after only a few paces in. I counted my steps, and I had passed two-thousand steps long ago.

By the time I contemplated putting Mariella down, so I could at stretch, the first signs of light glimmered. A tiny dot, but it was light, and that meant we were getting close.

Almost in answer to my hurried steps, something scuttled across the ceiling of the tunnel. As fast as I could, I shifted Mariella to my shoulder, unsheathed my knife, stabbed upward, and re-sheathed my knife as I stepped forward.

Something hit the ground behind me.

Not for the first time I thanked my training.

Especially now, when I had something, someone precious to protect.

Even more determined, I pushed forward.

When we finally left the tunnel, I was amazed by the sight before me.

The town spread out once out of the tunnel.

I knew the humans on this planet were industrious and unique from other races we had met.

But to have constructed something like Glymna - it made them capable of such great beauty.

Glymna was a remarkable town. All but two buildings were carved into the mountain itself, with what looked like two small utility sheds outside. As more light began illuminating the area, I saw more and more of the town. It seemed as if the ground level was reserved for the more business-like portion of the town.

Based on my quick research, I knew there to be a grocery, a tavern, a supply store, a library, and various other places of work, maybe a dozen. The second level of the town was cut into the mountain with what looked to be a substantial walkway carved in as well. There were stairs that seemed to bite deep into the rock face then turn back around to the edges. The railings at the edge of the upper walkway were carved out of the rock with three steel cables between each stone post.

The mountains served as a natural defense against the Xathi or any invading force. But to add to it, the town had erected gun posts throughout the mountain walls. They could be manned in a matter of minutes and their cross-fire capability would be formidable indeed.

I looked up to see three rope bridges extending from one side of the town to the other, and behind me there was even more. There were no businesses on the tunnel side of the mountain, but there were three levels of cut-outs with stairs between each level and another set of stairs going towards the top of the mountain.

The town of Glymna was amazing. This part of the valley with the tunnel entrance was only a hundred or so feet across, then stretched out for what seemed to be a couple of miles to my left. The road from the tunnel was well paved, each side lined with grass and flower bushes with small "intersections" connecting to each set of stairs. A covered walkway was in front of each building, and once I got a bit of a closer look, something remarkable stood out to me…each building looked to be hand carved.

I could have stood there and stared at the marvel of

architecture, but a soft sound from Mariella brought me out of my reverie.

Wasting no time, I activated my holo unit so that I would appear as just another human male, albeit larger and more muscular.

No doubt news that humans were not alone on this planet had reached Glymna, but I didn't want a repeat just yet of anti-alien sentiment similar to what others on our ship had encountered after the first Xathi attack.

I had to get Mariella into a bed, soon. I could initiate contact as an alien later. I made my way to what looked like the tavern and carried her in.

The interior of the tavern was simple. Not a lot of decoration, eight tables with three or four chairs each, and a small bar at the far side of the room. The smells of cooking breakfast wafted through the air, causing my stomach to grumble.

"Hey, she alright?" The innkeeper's voice was gruff, like he had been yelling a lot.

"She's very tired. Can we get a room?"

"I only have one room available at the moment, are you sure you..."

"We'll take it," I interrupted. She was getting heavy, as were the packs.

He tilted his head, gave me a nod and a sly smile, and grabbed a key from a nearby stand. "Okay, bring the pretty lady and follow me. So, what brings you two to Glymna?" He led us up a set of stairs.

I wasn't sure what to tell him, but a version of the truth wouldn't be too much. "She's trying to do some research on something or other, I'm just here to keep her safe."

"Ah, bodyguard duty. Have you had a chance to *guard* that body yet?" He chuckled at his own attempt at humor.

I was glad Mariella was in my arms or I would have hit him.

I gave him a human-like grunt as he led us to our room. He opened the door for us, slipped the key into my hand, and flashed me a smile as he chuckled his way back down the stairs.

I eased myself into the room and saw the one and only bed. With some exasperation, I laid Mariella down in the bed. I took the packs off and looked around the rest of the room. It was small, and sparse.

I could sleep on the floor. I'd certainly slept in more uncomfortable places.

But that would be away from Mariella, and something within me snarled at the thought.

I climbed into bed with her, trying to let her have as much of the bed as possible. I took some deep breaths, let myself relax, and closed my eyes.

I must have dozed off, because I never felt her move until she put her arm around me.

It felt perfectly natural being so close to her. There wasn't the slightest bit of discomfort.

I moved slowly until Mariella was laying on my arm, curled up against me.

I took a deep breath of her intoxicating smell and wondered to myself what I had been missing my whole life.

Before I knew it, I had fallen peacefully asleep, with Mariella nestled into my side.

MARIELLA

Before I even opened my eyes, I was aware of a deep ache in my limbs. My legs screamed in protest as I tried to stretch.

That's what I got for falling asleep in the Scrapper. If I'd stayed awake I could have at least stretched before going to bed.

I cracked opened my eyes to see a ceiling and walls of smooth reddish stone, carved with intricate images depicting various views of the city.

I'd always liked Glymna. I never spent as much time here as I wanted to in the past. I mostly came to view the private archives of a handful of other historians with a predilection for paper rather than digital.

I was last here a little over a year ago to collect a manuscript about the properties of plants in this region. For unknown reasons, the author had written her notes in a dead language from Earth and I'd been hired to translate.

I should look for the translated files in the library back on the ship, I decided. Jeneva would find them interesting.

Glymna was carved into the very mountain range. It was a forested area, but it was nothing like the lush jungles of the flatlands. The trees were shorter, their canopies sparser. As far as I knew, there was only one stream that trickled through the mountains. Everything here was built to conserve, even the buildings. A breathtaking, unique city, one I hoped the Xathi never came near.

Mind clearing from my half-awake musings, I became aware of a weight over my torso.

Tu'ver.

His arm lay across my body. He'd taken off the top half of his skinsuit, exposing the slate gray and faint glow of green circuits. With a featherlight touch, I traced a finger over the circuits.

I had been doing that a lot lately, but Tu'ver never seemed to mind. I hoped he would say something if he did. There was something soothing about following the patterns in his skin. Functional, but still beautiful.

I stretched, joints popping as I rolled towards him. If we had to do any climbing today, my body was not going to be happy about it. As I moved, I let my fingers continue their lazy trek across Tu'ver's skin.

The last thing I remembered from the night before was listening to the low rumble of the Scrapper's almost silent engine and the steady thrum of Tu'ver's heartbeat. I learned more about his people every day, but there was so much I didn't know.

What his heart like mine?

Did he feel things in the same way I did?

He was more reserved than the others, especially the Skotans and the Valorni. But when he did speak, the others always listened.

When it was just us, he was quick to make a joke and seemed to enjoy our pointless banter.

I could never thank him enough for what he did for Leena. Asking him to sneak onto the Xathi ship and find her was one of the hardest things I'd ever had to do. But he said yes without hesitation.

I traced up his arm, over his shoulder and across his chest. His breathing was slow and steady. My gaze wandered up to his face. To my surprise, he was awake and watching me.

"Oh!" I gasped, looking away as my cheeks flushed with embarrassment. "Sorry, I don't know what I was doing."

"It feels nice," Tu'ver said, his voice low and heavy. "Don't stop on my account."

"I-" I started, but I didn't know what to say.

Tu'ver placed his hand over mine and started moving my hand over his skin again. I sucked in a breath. Sometimes, when it was just the two of us talking or reading together, I had the urge to take his hand or lean against him. It felt second nature, as natural as breathing. But I always refrained. I never knew where he stood.

This seemed like a clue.

I'd been intimate with other men before. Human men, obviously. It hadn't been often. I'd always felt like something was missing, a connection. Something that made it all matter.

As I traced patterns across his skin, I felt like the only thing I was missing was more of him.

When I looked up at him again, he'd lowered his face closer to mine. As if driven by instinct alone, I stretched up, closing the distance between us and pressed my lips to his. I felt a small shockwave of surprise jolt through him.

Then he lifted his hand to grasp the back of my neck and pulled me deeper into his kiss.

I'd thought about what it would be like to kiss him before, in my room on the *Vengeance* during those brief moments just before I fell asleep when my thoughts were completely unrestrained. For some reason, I'd always imagined his lips to be cold.

But they were warm and solid.

Everything about him was warm and solid.

His arm snaked around the small of my back, pulling me in close. I could feel every muscular curve of his chest. I needed to feel more.

A few weeks ago, Leena and I had shared a bottle of Valorni spirits. She told me about some of the things she did with Axtin. She told me that when they were together it was more like fighting, but fun fighting. She told me about all the things they said to each other in bed that I never would've forced past my lips.

But with Tu'ver, I didn't feel the need to say anything. We'd always had an uncanny ability to understand each other without speaking, and this was no exception.

His eyes drilled into mine, gauging my consent until with no words he pulled us half-upright to lift my shirt over my head, leaving only the black band of fabric I wore to cover my breasts.

His hands against my back heated, their movements more urgent. As I wrapped my arms around his shoulders, I clung to him, sparks sizzling at his every touch.

He hissed in pleasure before taking my bottom lip between his teeth and biting gently, rolling us both until I lay back on the bed below him, exposed and open.

Wanting more.

I whimpered in protest when his lips left mine, but it quickly became a pleasurable sigh as he left a trail of kisses from my shoulder up to my ear.

"You are exquisite," he growled, one hand sliding up my body to brush against the bottom of my breasts.

He kneaded one through the fabric until my nipples tightened to rigid peaks, and I moaned in response.

As he leaned over me, nipping and sucking down my throat, something large and hard pressed into my leg.

Something very large and hard.

My mind stuttered, mentally working to grasp the size of him as his tongue traced the curve of my breasts. His hand had moved lower, tantalizingly close to my core.

I realized, as another shiver of pleasure ran through me, I could stay here all day. No, I could stay here forever.

But I couldn't.

Slowly, regretfully, I placed my hands on Tu'ver shoulders and forced some distance between us. He looked down at me, his black eyes smoldering though his brow wrinkled with concern.

"We really should get moving," I said, blushing. "We're technically deserting the *Vengeance* by being here."

"You're not," Tu'ver replied, sitting up. He didn't meet my gaze, instead his expression turned cold, remote. "Just me. But if it's what you want, we'll go."

"I never said it was what I wanted," I said with a sad smile.

What I wanted was to stay in this bed, with him. More than I'd ever wanted another man.

He knew that, didn't he?

"But it's the smart thing to do."

"Yes, of course," he agreed. He struggled to maintain his composure. "It was not my intention to distract you."

"There's nothing wrong with a distraction," I said, uncertainty creeping over me. Perhaps I'd misjudged this whole situation.

"Finding the information, you need for your research is important," he said with a nod.

I couldn't argue with that, but something didn't feel right. Did he regret what we'd just done? Should I have stopped it before it went too far?

Another thought formed as a cold stone of dread settled in my stomach.

Was it because I was human? Maybe he thought he wanted me but realized we were too different. I didn't know anything about K'veri women or how K'veri relationships worked. For all I knew, I could have done something offensive.

I wanted to say something, but my words failed me. Tu'ver was right about one thing. We had a job to do here, and the sooner we did it the better. We could sort out whatever this was between us later.

I fell back to my old motto.

If the universe wanted it, it would happen.

But somehow, it didn't bring me the comfort it once did.

TU'VER

I was ashamed of myself. Of my weakness.

We were here for a purpose. We had a mission.

And I'd been willing to delay it for my own wants, desires.

Soft, gentle Mariella showed more strength.

I would not let her down again.

We dressed in silence, and I turned on the holo unit before we left the room. From previous visits, she knew right where to go.

Despite my resolve to stay focused on the mission, my mind lost discipline, just from her nearness.

What was I looking for with her? Was I looking for something for right now? I quickly threw that thought out.

No.

The idea of being with Mariella as just a fling, for just short-term companionship, made me feel hollow, empty.

It was awkward for me to think of a relationship based on my emotions. It just wasn't something the K'ver did. Skotans married for life, but they let their emotions play a major role in their decisions.

Based on what I had learned from the ship's computer, as well as talking with the Skotan members of the crew, Vrehx's relationship with Jeneva could potentially last for years before they finally achieved a life-long bond. While raw emotions brought Skotan couples together for mating, those raw emotions were usually pent up for at least two or three years before they acted upon them. The fact that Vrehx had acted upon his feelings with Jeneva so quickly showed that either he was willing to be more "human" in his actions or his bond with her was already that strong. If he held to Skotan traditions, Jeneva would be the only woman in his life until his death.

The Valorni were even more human based on what I've seen. The Valorni were well known throughout our corner of the universe for their berserker rage and their emotional outbursts, and that carried over to their love making and mating bonds. They were notoriously boisterous, with the males and females both trying to dominate, and that somehow worked for them. Valorni were known for not being the most faithful of companions when it came to pleasure bonds, but when they did find their life-long connection, they would die and kill for their mate. Valorni history is full of stories of wars or battles fought over someone slighting someone's mate. Their emotions ruled more than reason, and it had led to several decades in Valorni history where their populations were sparse, and other decades where their population boomed nearly out of control. To see Axtin and Leena together was like watching a Valorni mating process. They were both volatile, hot-headed, and absolutely perfect for one another.

From what I could gather from the humans that I spoke with and observed, they were some weird mixture of Valorni and Skotan, with sometimes a little bit of K'ver mixed in. The women were the perfect example. Jeneva seemed to be a match for Vrehx...both letting their passions show when the time was right but being calm and discreet about it. Meanwhile, there were times I overheard Leena talking about what she had done to Axtin or vice versa, and she seemed happy to detail their actions.

I side-stepped a small animal of some sort as we made our way to the library. Mariella walked ahead of me at a slow pace, which seemed odd for someone that was so insistent on getting work done instead of spending time with me.

I shook my head, trying to push my emotions back down. K'ver were more logic oriented than Valorni or Skotan. It wasn't that we didn't have emotions or use them.

Rather we were all taught at a young age that letting our emotions get the better of us would lead to bad decisions and terrible lives. Our mating bonds focused on what would give us the best life and the most successful offspring. Most K'ver marriages were pre-arranged between families that had known one another for years or had been researched extensively. There were very few secrets in the K'ver culture, at least when it came to the idea of marriage.

While I had not yet been promised to someone, my sister, Cannira, had. I had never seen anyone as beautiful as my sister on her bonding day. Her smile seemed to light up the world, and I knew she was in love with not only the moment, but her mate as well. I wanted that. I wanted what she had...that joy, that lighter than air feeling, that pure happiness that came from being with someone you truly wanted to be with, that you felt you belonged with.

I looked at Mariella and considered. The ache in my chest was something that I hadn't felt since Cannira died, and I wasn't sure how to fix it.

I had failed her.

As we approached the library, Mariella's pace picked up a bit, and there was a bounce in her step. Just from that little skip, I could tell she was excited to get back to work. Work that might help her and Leena find a cure to their sickness.

I had to help her find what she needed. If I wanted anything like what Cannira had, if I wanted anything to happen for me, I had to help Mariella because she was the one that I wanted this life with. I think that was the seminal moment for me, when I finally acknowledged, without a doubt in my mind or my heart, that Mariella was the one I wanted to have that unity bond, that mating bond, that *life* bond with.

It was time to get to work.

MARIELLA

The Library of Glymna was amazing. Like all the other buildings here, the archive was hewn from the stone of the mountains. The shelves containing rows and rows of datapads, the tables, even the seats were carved from stone. The stone floor was covered in intricate rugs woven from threads of deep blue, ruby, and emerald. All the lights were designed to look as if they were firelit sconces embedded in the stone walls. Every seat had plush cushions and massive pillows were strewn about for comfortable reading. This was an archivist's dream.

One look at the cavernous room and I'd completely forgotten my worries over Tu'ver.

I found the librarian organizing a stack of paper documents on the other side of the room. While most documents were on data pads, and people had their own data pads of varying memory, capable of holding several hundred or just a few documents for various uses, along with data disks to transfer or store information not immediately needed to one's data pad, this library held a vast amount of paper records.

I saw sections of the library where paper records were being transferred to data disks, but it looked like a monumental task.

The librarian was nearly a full head shorter than I was and must have been the oldest person in the city. Her brown skin was etched with deep wrinkles. Her blue eyes crinkled with warmth when I approached.

The archivist and librarian community was tight-knit. While we'd corresponded in the course of my work, somehow, we'd never met in person.

"Hello, dear," she said. "Do you need help?"

"I was hoping I could access the original records from the first surveying expedition," I said, smiling sweetly. The librarian's eyebrows shot up in surprise.

"Those are very old, very rare documents, dear," she said warily, a polite refusal. "We're trying to preserve as much of the old paper documents until we can transfer them to disks."

I didn't let my smile falter.

"My name is Mariella Dewitt," I said brightly. "I'm an archivist myself. My grandmother was on the survey team and I was hoping to learn more about her. She died before I was born."

"Dewitt?" The librarian repeated. "Of course, my dear. Let me get them for you."

The librarian gathered her things and began to walk towards where the documents were stored.

"I hate doing that," I said after the woman was out of earshot.

"Why? You're getting what you need," Tu'ver replied. He wasn't as cold towards me as he was before, but something still didn't feel quite right. I tried not to focus on it.

"It feels dirty using my grandmother's name and death for personal gain," I explained.

"This personal gain could save your life," Tu'ver countered.

"I know. You're right," I said, biting the inside of my cheek. A few moments later, the librarian waddled over carrying a thick folder.

"This is all I have," she said, gently setting the folder on one of the stone tables. "Just let me know when you're finished, and I'll put it all away for you."

"Thank you," I said with a kind smile. I bent over the file, opening it gingerly and taking out the papers with the greatest care. Inside, there was an original photo of the survey team. My grandmother was smiling, as was Sidra's grandfather and great aunt.

I carefully sorted through the documents one by one, taking notes and pictures with my datapad frequently until I found something that gave me pause.

"Hey, look at this," I called quietly to Tu'ver, who was browsing a nearby shelf. He peered over my shoulder, looking at the map I'd found. It was hand drawn and geographically imperfect, but it was a map of the areas the survey team had worked on. The largest marked off area was exactly where Glymna stood now. There were a few other, smaller sights mapped out including one with a big red X over it.

"Whatever they discovered there couldn't have been good by the looks of it," Tu'ver said indicating the X-ed out area.

"I want to go see what it is," I said, snapping a few pictures of the map.

"You woke up late this morning and we've been here for six hours," Tu'ver reasoned. "If we go now, we could get stuck out in the mountains overnight and I don't want to risk that." I opened my mouth to protest but Tu'ver raised a hand to stop me. "We'll spend tonight coming up with a plan and we'll go first thing in the morning."

"Okay," I agreed, trying not to sound dejected. It was a reasonable plan. But a part of me was concerned, "Won't we be in trouble with the *Vengeance*?"

"They've been trying to send messages to discover

my location the for last few hours. They already know we're away," he said grimly. "Another day won't change anything. But if it gives us the time to complete our mission then the cost will be worthwhile."

"Thank you," I said to him sincerely. I had no idea that the ship had been trying to reach him. That Tu'ver would pay a price for helping me.

"Come on, let's head back to the tavern," Tu'ver said, helping me put all the documents back neatly in their file. "I have an idea."

"What's your idea?" I asked, holding the folder to my chest.

"You'll see," Tu'ver said with a small smile. I gave him a suspicious look before going to seek out the librarian.

I returned the folder and thanked her before rejoining Tu'ver. We walked in silence out the library.

"Srell," he muttered to himself.

I looked at him quizzically.

"The holo unit," he said as he noticed me. "I should have checked it's wiring again this morning. They're not supposed to be used for this long without charging. I can fix it, but there's no guarantee how long the repair will last without the proper tools."

"Shit," I agreed.

"You have the right idea," Tu'ver said back with a twinkle in his eye.

"It's my fault—" I began, trying to apologize for how long I had taken searching through the documents.

"Not to worry," he held up a hand. "These humans should be aware of aliens in their midst by now."

With that Tu'ver simply switched off the holo unit.

We slowly began to walk back through the city, earning curious looks from everyone we passed. The people of Glymna certainly knew about the Xathi invasion. Enough of the planet's communication links survived that they must have known about the other races aboard the *Vengeance*, the warriors fighting against the Xathi.

Leena had told me about the horrible people that attacked Axtin while they were in Duvest, blaming him for everything the Xathi did.

But as we crossed through town, it didn't appear that the people of Glymna had the same fears. It might have been that the war was still far away in their minds, but whatever the reason, I was grateful.

When we entered the tavern, it was much busier. Nearly every table and barstool were taken for the evening meal. They all turned to stare at us when we walked in.

"Greetings," Tu'ver said in a bright, friendly voice I'd never heard him use. "How are you all tonight?" His fluent use of the local language caused more than a few raised eyebrows but seemed to ease a bit of the tension.

Half of the patrons returned to their food and drink. The other half kept a wary eye on Tu'ver. But he paid them no mind, simply walked over to the tavern owner, a stocky man with a scruffy beard and tired eyes.

"I have a favor to ask," Tu'ver said, putting on a charming smile.

"What do you want?" The tavern owner replied gruffly. He seemed more annoyed by someone speaking to him than he did about Tu'ver's appearance.

"See that lovely young lady there?" Tu'ver said, gesturing to me. "She is famished, and I promised her a good meal. Now, everyone we asked said that this place is the absolute best in the city. We already know how comfortable your rooms are, so it wasn't hard to sell us. But you look rather crowded at the moment."

I tried not to let my shock show on my face. Who knew Tu'ver could be such a smooth operator when he wanted to be?

"What's your point?" the tavern owner asked, his voice less gruff under Tu'ver's flattery.

"I'm a fair cook, myself," Tu'ver said easily. "And I did promise the lady a meal. Let me use your kitchen to make something up for her. I'll pay for anything I use and it's one less table you have to worry about." The tavern owner looked Tu'ver up and down with a critical eye. He looked at me once as well before turning back to Tu'ver.

"Just don't break nothing and put everything back where you found it," he said.

"Thank you," Tu'ver grinned before beckoning me to him.

"How in the hell did you pull that off?" I whispered as Tu'ver led me into the kitchen.

"I told you, confidence is key," Tu'ver grinned. "I've done some espionage work in the past. Those skills come in handy much more frequently than you'd think."

"I believe it," I said, still surprised that the tavern owner let us back here. "So, dinner? That was your idea?"

"Are you not hungry?" Tu'ver asked.

"No, I'm starving actually," I said quickly. "I just didn't expect this. Where did you learn to cook? I can't imagine it was part of spy school."

"I've always indulged in cooking when I needed a chance to think," Tu'ver said, pulling ingredients from the cooling unit. "I even made meals in the galley during slow periods when I was in the military."

"What changed?" I asked.

"The Xathi," Tu'ver said, voice cold and remote. "Once they arrived there was no time for small pleasures."

"Oh," was all I could think to say.

"I was originally trained as a sniper," he continued.

He started slicing a root with speed and precision. "Espionage - spy school - came later."

"You didn't spy on the Xathi, did you?" I asked.

"No," Tu'ver said with a dry chuckle. "That's a death sentence if I ever heard one. No, I did a lot of intelligence work against the Skotan military. When it looked like our only option was to join forces, K'ver leaders wanted to know everything first."

"The Skotan and the K'ver were at war before the Xathi showed up, right?" I asked.

"Technically yes," Tu'ver said. "It never really felt like a full war though. It was more like a series of senseless skirmishes. It'd been going on since before I was born. Before my father was even born. I don't think anyone really remembers how it started. Everyone believes a different story."

"What do you believe?" I pressed. He passed me a chunk of whatever he was now chopping for me to taste. It was starchy and a little sweet. Delicious.

"I believe that we didn't know what real war was until the Xathi showed up," Tu'ver said, his voice heavy.

"I can understand that," I said. "No one on this planet has really experienced war yet. It's a young world. Our population is still too low for us to start turning against each other. Besides, it's that sort of thing that cost us our home world."

"This world was hopelessly unprepared for the

Xathi," Tu'ver sighed. "The weapon, the one that caused the rift to open… I hope you know that if any of us had thought that would happen we wouldn't have used it."

"I don't blame you, or anyone on the *Vengeance* for what happened," I said gently. "You were just trying to defend your own worlds."

"Thank you for saying so," Tu'ver said before returning to his prep work. The silence hung heavy in the air between us.

"So," I started, unsure of what to say. "Are you good with knives because you're a chef or because you're a soldier?"

"What do you think?" He grinned before going back to chopping.

Ever since Tu'ver brought me onto the *Vengeance*, I felt like I knew him. There was something comforting and familiar about him right from the start.

But now, after listening to everything he just told me, I realized there was so much more to him. I'd never wanted to know more about a person than I did him.

A tiny warning sensation flickered in me. The fact that I knew so little about him meant I could learn something I didn't like.

I shook away the thought. There wasn't anything Tu'ver could tell me that would make me think less of him.

I was sure of it.

TU'VER

After dinner I settled Mariella in the bedroom.

I wouldn't, couldn't stay with her. Not until the mission had been completed. A sleepless night was nothing new to me, and there was work to be done.

One of the tavern workers told me that instead of following the trail that went to the right from the bridge and then threw the tunnel, I could have gone left. A longer road but would lead back around to town eventually.

Most importantly, it was wide enough for the Scrapper.

Without Mariella in my arms and carrying only a small light, the trip through the tunnel went much faster. In the tunnel was the shriveled body of a giant brown spider. I stepped over it and continued.

I was back at the Scrapper in less than ten minutes. I started it up and followed the directions, and just as the worker had indicated, thirty yards to the left of the bridge was another, wider trail. It stuck close to the river gorge, and there was a time or two that my level of concern slightly rose as I was forced to get the Scrapper close to the edge to avoid a boulder, or some sort of bovine-like creature that refused to get out of my way.

I wondered what the meat of that creature would taste like but decided that shooting it just because it was obstinate was inappropriate, even if satisfying.

It made some sort of mewling crossed with a honking sound at me as I sped away.

The shorter trees of the mountain side were beautiful, and colorful enough to see even in the dim moonlight. They ranged from a bluish-grey coloring to green to orange and red. I slowed down to touch the needle-like leaves and found them to be very soft to the touch leaving behind a sweet scent on my fingers. I found myself sniffing at them several times as I made my way to the town road.

It didn't take long to find, and once I was on open road and knew where I was going, I opened her up and let the Scrapper fly. It didn't last long, but it was still a great way to wake up in the morning.

I glanced down at the console and noticed the

temperature gauge, it was apparently cold outside. It wasn't the first time I was grateful for my built-in circuitry, it kept me warm in this cool mountain air.

I parked the Scrapper just outside the tavern and went inside to wake Mariella. I found her in the room packing some food into a pack I hadn't seen before.

"Figured we could use something to eat while we were out," she said when she saw my raised eyebrow. "I borrowed a pack."

"Very good. The Scrapper's outside. It's cold right now, but it should warm up as soon as we get out of the mountain walls and into more open area," I said to her as I grabbed my pack and reached for my weapons.

"I'm pretty sure I can stay warm leaning up against you," she said with a smile. I smiled back at her as I double-checked my rifle.

"Are you ready?" I asked as I slung my rifle over my shoulder.

"Yep. Let's go."

I held the door open for her as she walked out, her hand lightly touching mine as she passed. We loaded up on the Scrapper, with Mariella leaning in tight against me.

It felt right, somehow.

Getting myself as comfortable as I could, I reached around her to grab the controls and started the Scrapper. With a tiny squeeze of my arms, I got us going. I could feel her shiver just a bit as we passed through the cold air, but I gave her another reassuring hug, trying to warm her up.

One minute, everything had a grayish hue to it thanks to the mountain blocking the sun, then suddenly it was bright as the sun topped the far peaks and started its rise in the sky.

Mariella peeked at the map she had taken a picture of and directed me towards two mountains off to our right. It was there that the red-X on the map would hopefully be.

Small fields of grass filled with Luurizi, a small stream with three of those bovine animals—that I later learned were called Kudzens—drinking from its moving waters. More of those colorful trees were ahead of us and to our right, and some breaks in the mountains showed us the plains we had raced through on our left.

The country was beautiful. But wouldn't be once the Xathi arrived.

Judging from where we were on the map and the speed of the Scrapper, we decided to stop and eat some of the breakfast Mariella had packed. It wasn't bad, a little too much spice for this meal in my opinion, but it did what it was supposed to do, fill us up.

Mariella talked a bit about the lost human world. Human history wasn't far off from K'ver history in terms of constant battles and general ability at ignoring history's lessons.

However, humans had been unable to save their home from themselves and had spread out into space, finding new homes where they hoped to make new beginnings and better stories.

After breakfast, I offered to show her how to use the Scrapper, telling her that it would be beneficial to both of us as a "just in case" scenario.

"I'm not sure that's a great idea," she said nervously.

"Give it a try," I reassured her. "I'm right here. What could go wrong?"

Apparently, everything.

After the third time we had to dodge away from a tree I took the controls back. "It's fine. It's my fault for trying to teach you with both of us on it. The Scrapper's made for one person, and with both of us, it's harder to control. You did very well."

"If you meant that, you'd promise to teach me again when we got back to the Vengeance," she said with a sly smile.

I swallowed hard, remembering the last tree coming at us very, very quickly. "I don't lie to you," I promised. But I might have a few rotations of extra duty coming up before I had any free time.

As we came over a tiny rise, I pulled the Scrapper up to a stop and we looked down into the valley below. Rocky, with no trees and very little grass, and it looked as though several boulders of varying sizes had fallen from the mountains and cliffs above to decorate the valley below.

There were several ravines, many of them box canyons with only one entrance, and it all looked like a terrible maze below us. We spent several minutes looking down at the valley and the trail that led down to it, trying to find the best way through.

Finally, Mariella pulled on my arm and pointed towards a cave at the intersection of the two mountains that surrounded this valley, and it wasn't far away. The rock around it was a darker color than the surrounding area, glinting in the morning sunlight.

Luckily, there was also a trail that went around most of the maze-like valley floor that looked like it would bring us within walking distance of the cave.

I maneuvered the Scrapper down the valley and we made our way quickly to the end of the trail we wanted. It was maybe a hundred yards to the cave entrance, but it was a hundred yards of rock, gravel, boulders, and debris from what looked to have been several rock slides over the years.

We made our way up, making sure to find stable places to place our feet as we made our way up the hill.

"Mariella, let me go first."

But she didn't hear me, didn't listen, wrapped up in

her thoughts as we approached the cave. The maddening woman was more like her sister than either one of them cared to admit.

"Hold on," I called up to her as I clambered my way up the hill. "We don't know what's in that cave."

Her breathing was hard, and her bright eyes betrayed her excitement. This was something that could lead her to her answers, and we were only a few short steps away.

"Come on!" she insisted as she grabbed my arm. I shook my head and let her pull me, amused with her impatience.

The wide mouth of the cave looked as though it narrowed quickly. There didn't seem to have been much in the ways of excavation through the dark rock. As a matter of fact, I didn't see much bracing in the cave past the entrance and the first few feet.

Mariella didn't notice, didn't care, just rushed through looking for her answers.

A few steps in, my atmospheric sensors went ballistic, blaring out alarms and warnings. Without a thought, I wrapped my arms around Mariella and dragged her out of the cave at a run.

"What are you doing? What's going on?" she asked me in a huff as I set her down.

"My sensors are going crazy," I explained. "There's

something wrong with the air in there. Let me send you preliminary data."

A few seconds later, I had sent her my readings to her data pad.

With wide eyes, she stared at the what was showing up on her screen. With her hand covering her mouth, she looked at me, fear stamped on her face.

"Is there any way you can save those recordings? Maybe Leena could do something with them."

I nodded, then pressed a few buttons, saving the readings my sensors had made from our walk up to the cave as well as inside the entrance.

If the readings were that off the charts just inside the cave mouth, any deeper in would certainly be lethal without the proper gear.

And if the early colonists hadn't had my level of sensors, they might not know until it was too late.

I looked up from my arm pad and saw Mariella staring at the cave. I turned her to face me. "We need to go back to the *Vengeance* now. The ship has proper ventilated breathing gear and detoxification suits. We need to do a full recon to see what else we can find," I said to her as she stared, gnawing on her lip. "Besides, we now have a clue. With this, General Rouhr is more likely to authorize a proper expedition and we'll sort this out. I believe we're ready to return."

Mariella looked at me for a long moment, weighing everything I had said.

"Agreed." She nodded, lips pressed to a thin line. "Come on. The sooner we get back, the sooner we can start convincing him." She turned away from the cave and started walking back to the Scrapper.

I watched her for a few paces, marveling at her persistence.

Her disappointment at this setback was evident, but she wouldn't give up.

Sweet Mariella was a warrior.

As she changed direction to go around a boulder, she let out a shriek.

The boulder moved.

Apparently, what we had thought was rock when we walked up was some sort of creature.

"What the koso is that thing?" I yelled as I rushed to her.

"I don't know. It looks like a damn stone bear!" was her response as she kept scrambling away from the thing.

I didn't know what a bear was, but if it was anything like this thing, I could imagine her fear. It raised itself up on its back haunches, a solid twelve to thirteen feet in height and looked as if it could make the entire strike team an easy meal.

I knew there was nothing I could do to it with my

knife, and there was no way I could use my rifle on this shifting ground.

But it was far too focused on Mariella.

I picked up a rock and threw it at the beast. It was a lucky throw, I must have hit it in its face, I suppose, because it turned its attention to me.

"RUN!" I yelled at Mariella as I grabbed another stone and threw it. The beast roared at me, dropped down to all four feet, and charged. Instinct took over.

I knew I had to get it away from Mariella, so that's what I did.

I turned and ran, not fast enough to get away, but not slow enough to be caught. As I ran I scooped up rocks and turned to throw them, keeping its attention focused on me.

I led it down into the valley, its roars and ground-shaking charge pushing me on. I took a turn down one of the many canyons, looking back to make sure it was still following me.

The beast was still coming, its claws digging gouges into the ground as it pursued me. The paws themselves were the size of my chest, the claws as long as my blade, hilt and all.

As I round a small bend in the canyon, it stopped a few yards ahead of me, and the walls stretched over a hundred feet over my head. I was trapped.

I reached the end of the canyon and turned to face

the creature. If it was away from Mariella, that was the only thing that mattered.

I quickly sent a copy of the atmospheric readings to the computer on the Scrapper, so Mariella would have them, then braced myself for what was sure to be my last fight.

"Shit!" I gasped. I couldn't see Tu'ver anymore. I couldn't hear fighting. "Shit, shit, shit!" I needed to think. Why couldn't I think?

I needed to help Tu'ver. That thing could tear him to shreds.

What if it already did? No, no I couldn't let myself think like that. Tu'ver was smart, strong, and armed. I'd seen him fight before.

And from the way Axtin talked about his abilities when Tu'ver boarded the Xathi ship to locate Leena, I felt confident that Tu'ver would be able to hold his own until I figured out what to do. I just needed to think.

I wished I could talk to Leena right now. She thrived under pressure. She could make decisions quickly and confidently. I didn't work like that. I needed to see the possibilities sketched out. I needed to think through every possible eventuality.

Going back to Glymna was not an option.

The only other thing I could do was follow the trail of the creature as it tore after Tu'ver.

I picked my way over the rocky terrain as quickly as I could manage. Tears blurred my vision. I slipped, scrapping the entire length of my forearm on a jagged slab of rock.

"Damn it!" I sobbed. What the hell was I even doing? I'd never been a fighter. I didn't even have a weapon. I should've thought about that. I should've thought this whole, stupid half-baked idea through before dragging Tu'ver out here. I should've never asked him to leave the *Vengeance*. If anything happened to him, it would be my fault.

The thought of losing Tu'ver was so unbearable that my heart felt heavy and my chest felt like it'd been smashed with a stone. My mind spun, desperate for anything that would save him.

Occasionally, Jeneva and I had talked about the creatures that populated the denser jungle in the flatlands. As I stumbled over rocks and tree roots, I fought to remember anything useful Jeneva had said to me.

The thing that attacked us ambushed us. It blended in perfectly to the environment. A lot of the living trees in the jungle did the same thing. Jeneva said that was because they weren't built to chase after their prey for long. Assuming the same principle was at work here, if Tu'ver and I could make a break for it, the rock beast might not be able to catch us if we could just keep running long enough.

However, I was reminded that the rocky terrain wasn't suitable for racing as I lost my footing for the third time.

This time, I managed to right myself without leaving a layer of skin on the rockface. Between the steep inclines and the ground constantly shifting beneath my boots, I doubted Tu'ver and I could move fast enough to get away from the rock beast.

The more I thought about it, the more depressing the reality of the situation felt.

But giving up wasn't an option.

Leena needed me and the information we'd found.

The Vengeance needed Tu'ver.

And damnit, so did I.

I clamored over another ridge and was equal parts distressed and delighted to hear conflict. The sound of metal clashing with stone echoed through the slopes of the valley. Feeling hopeful, I scrambled up another small ridge.

It was more difficult to climb than the previous ones were. The ridge was more like a loose pile of rocks rather than a geographical fixture. I reached up, grabbing for a large rock that looked sturdy enough for me to use for leverage, but it came loose.

I slid back down the ridge, bringing half of the stones and pebbles with me. High above me, rocks slipped down the ridge to fill in the space vacated by the stone I'd grabbed for. It looked like half of the very mountain was shifting to accommodate for the loss.

Forced to restart my climb, I chose a different route. I hauled myself up a crooked tower of larger rock slabs until I was able to see over the top of the ridge. Tu'ver was far below me on the canyon floor, his back pressed against a flat rock face the size of a small house. The rock beast had him cornered.

I nearly called out for him but clamped a hand over my own mouth to silence myself. The last thing I wanted was to break Tu'ver's focus. He was caught up in a complicated dance of parry and retreat with the rock beast. His knives bounced off the beast with each strike, creating small showers of sparks, not seeming to bother the creature at all.

Tu'ver's advantage was in his speed. The rock beast, though it's blows would crush bone into dust, was not very agile.

And from the looks of it, not very smart. Tu'ver moved in a pattern of four or five different techniques and the beast could not anticipate his next move.

I bit the inside of my cheek to prevent myself from crying out when the rock beast's flinty claws scrapped along the vertical rock face just inches from Tu'ver's head. I forced myself to look away. I couldn't think straight if I kept watching.

Now that I found Tu'ver I had a new objective. With no weapons, I would be useless in this fight. Perhaps I could distract the rock beast. Tu'ver's strength was in ranged weapons. If I got the rock beast far enough away for one of Tu'ver's long-range guns to be effective...

The rock beneath my right foot shifted and slipped out from under me. I gracelessly landed on my backside and grasped whatever I could to stop myself from sliding into the valley with Tu'ver and the rock beast.

Again, the side of the mountain practically rearranged itself. Rocks many feet above me slipped down into the valley. Some of the smaller rock chips and pebbled below me slid so far down they spilled onto the valley floor.

These minor rockslides were easy to set off.

I looked up, shielding my eyes from the glaring sun that would soon duck behind the mountain peaks. Bathed in a patch of yellow-gold sunlight, as if it wanted me to notice it, an enormous boulder precariously perched on the side of the mountain. One well-placed disturbance would send it crashing down, likely bringing half the mountain with it.

It was our only shot at getting out of here alive.

I selected a few rocks, choosing carefully so that I would not trigger another small slide. I palmed one of them and, with a silent wish, lobbed it at the rock beast. It fell short, shattering about fifteen feet behind the beast's legs.

It took no notice.

But Tu'ver did. His eyes darted to me, as he dodged another onslaught of claws.

"Mariella, get out of here," he shouted.

"No! I have a plan!" I shouted back, hoping that my voice might do what the rock I threw failed to do. The rock beast faltered but still wasn't convinced there was better prey to peruse.

I lobbed another rock, this time landing much closer to my target. The rock shattered just to the left of the beast, close enough for rock chips to bounce off its body.

My third stone hit its target.

It shattered over the back of the rock beast. It paused, lifting its disproportionately small head and looked around for its attacker.

"Over here!" I hollered, throwing a smaller rock. This time I hit it square in the face. I don't think I caused it any pain, but I did piss it off.

It roared in outrage, turning away from Tu'ver as it searched for its attacker. It still didn't see me up on the ridge. This thing was dumber than...well, a pile of rocks.

"Mariella!" Tu'ver shouted, drawing the rock beast's attention once more.

"Damn it, Tu'ver!" I screamed, my voice echoing off the mountainside. "Just trust me!" I tossed a few rocks in rapid succession until the rock beast figured out where I was. It snarled, its beady eyes fixating on me.

"Your plan doesn't seem very well thought out," Tu'ver shouted back. The rock beast paused, looking back at him, but ultimately decided I might be easier prey.

Excellent.

Except for the part that I probably really was an easier snack.

It crawled along the rubble toward me, and I forced myself to stand fast.

"When this stony bastard is at the foot of the ridge, shoot!" I instructed, pointing ahead. Finally, Tu'ver seemed to understand. He nodded once before reaching for his sniper rifle.

There was a large chance this plan wouldn't work at all. The boulder might not tumble the way I want it to. Tu'ver might miss.

No, that was ridiculous.

He wouldn't miss.

Since the creature was made of rocks, there was a

good chance a rock slide would do nothing to harm it. I'd say the odds of the rockslide crushing myself and Tu'ver to death were not in our favor.

But it was too late to change course now. The rock beast was creeping toward me, keeping its body low. I just needed it to get a little bit closer, right up against the base of the ridge.

Its hindquarters dropped. It was going to pounce.

"Now, Tu'ver!" I shouted.

The rock beast leaped forward.

The crack of a bullet striking stone erupted in the air.

At first, nothing happened. The rock beast paused, looking at me as if it were trying to figure out how I made such a noise.

Beneath my feet, the mountain shuddered. I didn't want to take my eyes of the rock beast, even as I heard the first crash of the dislodged boulder tumbling toward me. The stones at my feet began to shift as they were pushed downward. Pebbles and small chips of rock stung as they bounced off me.

"Get up as high as you can!" I yelled to Tu'ver. If he climbed high enough up the opposite side of the valley, he would be safe from the rockslide.

I, however, didn't have as many options. The massive boulder was picking up speed, sweeping up more and more as it toppled.

The rock beast finally noticed the avalanche of solid stone pummeling toward it. It darted down the valley, soon out of sight.

I glanced around looking for Tu'ver. He was almost directly across from me on the other side of the valley, watching in horror as the waterfall of stone crashed closer and closer.

At least he was safe.

Out of options and out of time, I jumped.

TU'VER

What in the ketonsin was that woman thinking? I was grateful she had given me a chance to breathe, but she was supposed be safe in the sled. Then she yelled at me to shoot at a rock and I knew what her plan was. It was a clever plan at that.

I couldn't waste the few seconds of time she'd bought. I unstrapped my rifle, cocked it, took aim, and fired, all in less than two heartbeats. My aim was true, and the canyon soon echoed with loud cracking noises as the boulder broke free.

I re-slung my rifle and sprinted towards the far side of the canyon. I had made it maybe fifteen or twenty yards when the air was split with a thundering crack. The noise ricocheted down the walls, each strike against the canyon walls or an outcropping sending more noise into the air, reverberating off the walls of the canyon and into my ears. I felt deaf as I looked back to see what was happening.

The boulder slammed into the ground close to the creature, knocking it over. A quick glance up showed a shower of rocks and dirt following the massive boulder, and more parts of the canyon wall breaking away. I looked to the top to see Mariella fall out of sight as the canyon wall gave away, sending a great cloud of dust and rocks right at me. I turned and ran like I had never run before.

There was a collection of boulders fifty yards ahead big enough to shield me, so I hoped. I willed myself to run faster, but I could already feel pellets and small rocks hitting me from the back. The cloud of dust covered me before I got close and cut off my sight of everything. The dust clogged my lungs, my eyes filled with dust, and my ears were ringing with the non-stop thundering, cracking, and rumbling of the rock slide.

A boulder as big as me landed and rolled past me as another brushed against my shoulder, knocking me off balance. Somehow, I managed to keep my footing and ran, coughing and choking along the way.

I forced myself to keep breathing through the dust and grime.

I had to find Mariella.

I was supposed to keep her safe.

She shouldn't have been out here in the first place. I don't know why I let her talk me into coming on this poor excuse for an expedition.

If anything happened to her, I would never forgive myself.

I reached where I thought she'd fallen, but she was nowhere to be found.

Where was she?

"Mariella?" I called for her, my voice echoing sharply off the canyon walls. "Mariella!"

No answer.

Only the quiet noise from the rocks finally settling.

A deep ache settled in my chest as if someone had my heart in a vice grip.

I couldn't admit that there was a possibility that she was-No! I wasn't going to go there.

She was here.

I would find her.

I tore at the rock pile beneath me. Sharp pieces of stone cut into my palms and wedged themselves under my fingernails, but I didn't care.

"Tu'ver," I finally heard a small voice call, not from beneath the stones but from farther down the canyon. I stopped, hoping I hadn't imagined it.

"Mariella," I called, scanning every nook and cranny of the canyon for a sign of her.

"I'm here!"

She was somewhere below me. I threw down the bolder I'd been trying to lift and rushed down the canyon wall.

Her hand grasped for purchase on a rock about thirty feet from me. I leaped down to a large, flat rock that created a small plateau when it tumbled down the mountainside.

Clever girl.

As the rocks had started to come down, she had found an overhang.

It saved her life.

"I've got you," I said, hauling her up.

"I didn't think I would fall so far," she admitted. "Maybe I didn't think that all the way through."

Her face was marred by a few superficial scrapes, her hair and clothes coated in dust.

But she was fine and whole.

Once she was on solid ground, I pulled her tightly against my chest, willing my own heart to beat again, now that she was with me.

She winced slightly.

"Are you hurt?" I asked, running my hands over her limbs, checking for injury.

"I don't think anything's broken," she replied. "I think I dodged a bullet there."

"They were boulders," I corrected, "Not bullets."

"I owe you my life for that distraction." I tucked a

strand of hair behind her ear. "Don't do that again." I wrapped my arms around her more gently this time, resting my chin on top of her head. "I'd rather fall down a thousand mountains than feel that sort of fear again."

"That's how I felt when you ran off with that rock monster," She said, leaning into me sideways. "I felt so helpless. I didn't know what to do. I was so scared you'd be dead when I caught up to you."

"I'm not going anywhere," I promised. "Someone's got to keep an eye on you."

She looked up at me then, the most beautiful creature I had ever laid eyes on. I brought my lips to hers, kissing her like she kissed me the day before. I felt her body relax into me as one of her hands reached up to touch the side of my face.

When my species formed mating bonds, love was not the deciding factor.

Desire didn't come into the equation.

And all of that was tossed to the side in the face of what I felt with Mariella.

I wound my hands into her hair. She twisted in my arms until she faced me, her breasts pressing into my chest.

I could almost feel her heart pounding, or perhaps it was my own. Adrenaline from the fight, the knowledge that I'd almost lost her, pushed me over the edge.

Sliding my hands down her curves I sank my fingers

into her hips, then lifted her, bringing her face level with mine. Her legs automatically wrapped around my waist, and I couldn't resist dragging her core against me until she moaned, eyes wide and rolling.

I spied another flat rock nearby, it's smooth surface and sheltered location perfect for what I had in mind. When we reached it, I held her with one arm, reaching behind me with the other to pull the top half of my skin suit off, smoothing it over the hard surface.

Setting her on the edge of the rock, I ran my fingers along the hem of her shirt.

"This has to go, babe."

She lifted her arms, and once it was off I quickly rolled it into a pillow. Next, that fascinating black band, and the tempting flesh it hid.

Mariella traced patterns over my shoulders and down my arm and I shuddered. No one's touch had ever affected me like this.

Brushing my thumb over the black fabric I reveled in her parted lips and hazed glance.

"This too?"

"I think you'd better," she agreed.

Luscious breasts freed, I bent over them, licking and teasing one tight bud while rolling the other between my fingers.

Her heartbeat increased, her breathing grew more irregular with ever touch. I laid her down gently, cupping the back of her head with my hand until she was stable on the rock.

"Lift up, sweetheart."

I pushed her back until she was lying flat against the rock and tugged off her leggings and the pair of black undergarments in one swift motion. I paused for a moment just to admire her, beautiful and naked, surrounded by the harsh face of the canyon.

Logic and reason meant nothing.

She was a goddess, my goddess.

Returning my attention to her breasts, her throat, her lips, I let one hand drift lower, stroking and teasing until I reached the silken skin of her inner thighs.

"Tu'ver, please," she panted, arching off the rock.

Thankful for my curiosity after Axtin and Vrehx had found human mates, I skimmed over her slick folds, circling the swollen nub of her clit with my thumb.

She whimpered and squirmed against me, but I was far too intoxicated by her pleasure to rush anything.

A second, a third stroke and then I slipped two fingers inside her.

With a gasp she half-sat from the rock, arms wrapped around my neck. Her open mouth was an invitation to taste her again, her moans and gasps spurring me harder.

As she shuddered through her release, I lowered her to the rock, stroking her side, watching her breath.

"Tu'ver," she murmured, "I want more."

By all the Void, I'd never have enough of her either. I leaned away to ease out of my pants, but with deft hands, she reached for me, revealing the hard length of my rigid cock.

She blinked in surprise and only faltered for a moment before taking me in her mouth.

I tipped my head back, hissing through clenched teeth. This was not a part of the pleasure I'd anticipated. I could have stood there forever, letting her use her perfect lips and tongue.

But it wasn't enough. I wanted to claim her. I was as hard as the rock I'd perched her on, literally aching for her.

She began to run her tongue up and down the length of my shaft, looking up at me and I swore by all the systems in the universe that I had never loved anyone or anything as much as this.

But I wanted more.

"Not this time," I ground out through gritted teeth as I eased her back. "I need to be inside of you, now."

"Then take me," she whispered back. That was all I needed to hear. She'd awoken something primal within me, a creature filled with lust and need.

· · ·

I PULLED her in as close as I could. Her skin was so soft against mine. I snaked one hand around her back holding her against me as I rocked my hips against her.

The head of my cock bumped against her opening and I froze, not wanting to hurt her.

"Please," she whispered again, and then rocked against me.

That was my undoing. I plunged into her.

Her eyes fluttered closed as I thrust into her. I gripped her hips, pulling her hard against me as I watched the sway of her breasts and her pretty mouth gasp in pleasure.

If this was the last thing I ever experienced, I would die happy.

"Look at me, sweetheart," I managed, then lost myself in her eyes as they darkened, lost focus as I steadily drove within her.

Her cries echoed off the canyon as she reached the apex of her pleasure. Her climax broke something in me and I lost control, pounding into her like a wild thing until she crested again while I roared my release.

I leaned forward, gasping at the intensity of it.

Mariella panted as well, her breasts rising to rub against my chest each time she took a breath.

I kissed her hard before rolling off to her side. She immediately curled up against me, a blissful smile on her face. I wrapped my arms around her and kissed the top of her head.

I wasn't sure how long we laid there. There was a large possibility that we both dozed off, spent and warmed by the rock beneath us. It wasn't until a light breeze blew through the canyon and Mariella shivered against me that sanity returned.

I found Mariella's clothes first and handed them to her before pulling on my own. The moment we got back to the *Vengeance* I planned on pulling her into my cabin indefinitely.

"What were we doing before this?" Mariella asked, a dreamy look in her eyes.

"Disobeying orders to go on a dangerous personal quest," I replied.

"Oh, right. We better get back to that," she giggled.

MARIELLA

I couldn't stop smiling as Tu'ver and I made our way back towards where we left the Scrapper. My skin felt warm and flushed, my body practically singing.

Every time Tu'ver touched my waist or pulled me closer to help me navigate the tricky terrain, it was all I could do not to melt and beg him to take me again.

For the first time in years, I was excited about something other than books and research. I'd never felt like this before.

Yes, there was the rush of excitement, the shot of adrenaline, that came with starting something new. But there was also a sense of deep comfort. I knew Tu'ver, he knew me. He'd already shown me, in so many ways, that he was here for me.

Tu'ver hopped off a rock ledge and turned back to look up at me.

"I'll catch you," he offered, holding his arms out. I jumped down without a second thought, landing smoothly in his arms. He dipped his head, pressing his lips to mine in a kiss I wished could last forever. I made a low, whimpering sound when he pulled away.

"You're maddening, you know that?" He said, before kissing me once more. I smiled against his lips.

"It's not my fault you're a pushover," I teased, when he pulled back for the second time.

"I'm not a pushover. You're my weakness and you know how to exploit it," he replied. He clutched me close to his chest as he navigated the uneven footing.

"You can put me down now," I said, even as I let my head rest against his shoulder.

"The terrain is not flat yet," he said, offhandedly. "Besides, a mountain just fell on you. You've earned some time off your feet."

"A mountain didn't *fall* on me," I giggled, running my fingers lightly along his arm.

"From where I was standing, it sure looked like it did," Tu'ver replied. "If you think I'm letting you out of my sight ever again, you are very mistaken."

"I don't have a problem with that in any way whatsoever," I grinned.

"And you're definitely not going to be in charge of plans," Tu'ver added with a smirk.

"Excuse me, my plan was brilliant and worked flawlessly," I argued playfully.

"Your plan nearly stopped my heart," Tu'ver said. "And your previous plans don't have a much better track record. Need I remind you that you strolled into a cave seeping with toxic gas?"

"How was I supposed to know?" I shrugged in defense. "But you make a fair point. I'll leave the planning to you from now on."

"Thank you, dearest," Tu'ver said, pressing a kiss into my forehead.

The Scrapper was right where we left it, tucked between two large rock formations just outside the city. With me still in his arms, Tu'ver stepped into the tiny transport unit and lowered himself into the seat. It was still a tight fit. I knew my legs were going to be stiff when we made it back to the *Vengeance*. But I relished being so close to him.

Tu'ver powered up the Scrapper and gently guided it out from between the rock formations until we were high above the mountain rage. I peered down at the city below us, or rather the approximate area of where the city was. Glymna blended so seamlessly with the environment that, from up here, it was impossible to distinguish the natural structures from the carved ones.

"I hope we can come back some day," I mused, resting my head against Tu'ver's chest. He wrapped an arm around me, using the other to pilot.

"I'll do my best to ensure that happens," he swore. Smiling, I pressed my lips against his neck, making a trail until I saw goosebumps rise on his skin.

"Careful now," Tu'ver warned, his voice a low growl in my ear. "Keep that up and you'll be in trouble when we get back." He nipped my ear gently.

"If that's meant to deter me, it's not going to work," I purred in response. "Lucky for you, I literally cannot move an inch in this damn Scrapper."

"Unlucky for me, really," Tu'ver corrected.

"Aw, don't you worry," I crooned. "As soon as we're back on the *Vengeance,* you'll be very lucky indeed."

"Assuming General Rouhr doesn't have me shot on sight for technically stealing a Scrapper," Tu'ver added dryly. "And desertion."

"Right," I said with a wince. "You should let me talk to him. It's my fault for dragging you out here in the first place."

"You saved me from a rock monstrosity, now you're going to save me from my commanding officer?" Tu'ver chuckled.

"You saved me from the rock beast first and you saved me from noxious gas. Plus, you helped Axtin save Leena's life, so I still owe you," I countered.

"You don't owe me anything," Tu'ver said in a much softer voice. "I'd do anything to keep you safe." He kissed the top of my head. I smiled, too filled with joy to say anything else.

I was expecting to see General Rouhr, Vrehx, and maybe a few others waiting for us when we pulled the Scrapper into the docking bay. But no one seemed to notice our arrival. Everyone was running around, shouting into radios and it all looked very purposeful.

Something had happened, and we were walking into the middle of it.

"What's going on?" I asked as Tu'ver helped me out of the Scrapper.

"I'm not sure," he said. He looked uneasy. "I did not acknowledge the transmissions from the *Vengeance* to my internal receiver for fear of giving away our location. If I had received them they would have pinpointed our location and sent a party after us."

I looked around. There was panic in the air.

"Here, take this and go find your sister," he instructed, pressing the device containing the information on the gas from the cave.

"But—" I protested, but Tu'ver cut me off.

"I'll come find you once I know something. Understood?" He said.

"Okay," I agreed, but I wasn't happy about it. He

kissed my forehead before dashing off towards another part of the ship.

I tucked the device into my pocket and hurried towards Leena's lab, trying not to collide with the many rushing bodies. When I rounded the corner of the hallway that would take me to the lab, I almost collided head on with Leena.

"Mari?" Leena sputtered, her eyes a little wild. "Where the hell have you been?"

"Long story," I said, not quite meeting her steely gaze. "What's going on?"

"Oh, no," Leena said, gripping my upper arm and leading me back to her lab like I was a child she wanted to scold in private. "You answer questions first. Then I'll fill you in." Once inside the lab, she turned to me. She crossed her slender arms and gave me the piercing look that always made me crumble.

"Leena, please..." I began but she cut me off.

"This was a bad time for a romantic getaway, Mari!" she yelled.

"Tu'ver and I went to Glymna," I said, already prepared for the yelling.

"Wait?" Leena asked, disarmed. "What?"

"Didn't you get my note?" I said. "I left you one! I wouldn't just run off without telling you."

"No, I didn't get your note," Leena snapped, eyes

rolling. "Besides, Glymna is only passable by going through Xathi territory. That's not possibly safe!"

"It's my life too and I didn't want to put you in danger," I said defensively. "I was doing research in the library and I found something that might be related to our illness."

"What did you find?" Leena asked, all anger rapidly vanishing from her expression.

"Tu'ver and I found a cave teeming with an incredibly toxic gas," I said, pulling out the device with all the information we gathered and sliding it across the table to Leena. "The cave was on the original survey map. There was a big red X through it."

"So, this could be N.O.X?" Leena said, a grin spreading across her face.

"That's what I'm thinking," I said, unable to contain my own smile.

"This is amazing, Mari," Leena said. "But still...why go without talking to me first? I would have come with you. I have more experience with the Xathi than you."

"I wanted you to know that finding a cure matters to me," I shrugged. "Though I'll admit it, I did get a little carried away."

"I was too hard on you before," Leena sighed. "I shouldn't have lashed out the way I did. Everything you said was true."

"I know," I grinned.

"Don't push it," Leena laughed, walking around the table to hug me. I squeezed her tightly.

"Now, please tell me what's going on," I said when we broke apart. The nervous, wild-eyed look I'd seen on her face before rushed back.

"Something fell through the rift. Something big," she said. "From the scans, it looks like it could be another ship."

"Another Xathi ship?" I asked, a stone of dread sinking deep into the pit of my stomach. If another Xathi ship came through the rift, I didn't know what we would do. The *Vengeance* crew was already overwhelmed trying to handle one Xathi ship. The human population, my people, had already suffered greatly. Another Xathi ship would mean the end of our world entirely.

"They aren't sure," Leena shrugged. From the dejected way she held herself, I knew she shared my worries. "Axtin saw the scans himself. He said it doesn't look anything like the first Xathi ship."

"That's a good sign, isn't it?" I asked, trying to sound hopeful.

"Maybe. Maybe not. Xathi are known for absorbing useful things from other races," Leena shrugged.

"Oh," I said, weakly. "What's General Rouhr going to do?"

"He's mobilizing the strike teams for a recon

mission," Leena said. "The senior crew is going out. I think they were mentioning Tu'ver. You might want to see him. I know Axtin is going. He's actually excited to go. He's been getting restless. Not enough things to smash with his hammer around here I guess," she said dryly. My mouth fell open.

"I have to find Tu'ver," I cried, running from the lab before Leena could say anything else. I sprinted back to the docking bay. If the strike teams were getting ready to depart, they'd be there.

I didn't see anyone I knew, so I approached a Skotan barking orders into a commlink. He looked like he'd know what was going on.

"Excuse me," I said, switching to his own tongue. He turned, his brows raised in surprise. "Where's the strike team that's been assigned to the alien craft?"

"Deployed five minutes ago," he replied before turning his attention back to his commlink.

His words hit me like a blow to the chest.

Tu'ver and the rest of his strike team were already gone.

TU'VER

"If I didn't need you to assist the others in investigating the ship, I'd lock your srell of a body in the brig and feed you Xathi parts!!!" Rouhr yelled at me.

If he was starting to threaten me with Xathi as food, it meant he was running out of things to yell about.

"I apologize for my actions, sir. What I did was wrong, irresponsible, and against protocol. I acknowledge that. But I would do it again, sir. It was necessary for Mariella's and Leena's future, sir."

The look on his face was an interesting mixture of respect, anger, and sympathy. "One of these days, someone needs to explain to me what the situation is with those women, but right now is not the time. Report to Vrehx, immediately."

As I stood to leave, he stopped me. "Don't think I'm done with you Tu'ver. Your actions were beyond insubordination, and you will be disciplined accordingly."

With a nod and a salute, I said, "Yes, sir," and left the conference room. Leave it to my luck that just around the corner, waiting for me, was Sakev. He leaned against a wall, bright orange arms crossed across his thin, yet muscular orange chest. His spiked, bright red hair was a new look for him this week. His signature grin, always in place when he was in any mood other than angry, was bigger and more obnoxious than normal.

It bothered me. "What do you want?" I asked as I walked by.

He fell into step next to me. His amusement seemed to radiate from him. "Nothing really. I was just curious."

I tried to sound stern, "Curious about what?"

"I was trying to see if that human expression of 'if looks could kill' was real or not. Guess Rouhr just doesn't have that killer look, huh?"

"You're a ghee worm covered in srell." I turned down one of the halls and headed for the lift. I needed to get to Vrehx.

"Eh, I've been called worse. So, did Rouhr leave anything for you to sit on or was he just being loud?" Sakev asked as we stepped into the lift.

"My actions were wrong, and I acknowledge that. Captain Rouhr was merely letting me know that," I said as the doors closed. I pushed the button to go down and crossed my arms. Sakev had his head tilted as he looked at me, his infuriating smile getting bigger.

"Uh huh. Don't pull that srell with me, he ripped you several new ones," he said seriously. Then he laughed as he said "Well, at least you still got half a posterior to sit on."

"You're demented, you know that, Sakev?"

"Yep. That's why you guys love me."

"Why are you such a fool?"

He shrugged at me and smiled. "So, did you finally get a shot at Mariella? We had a wager started on whether you two would finally *come* together as one. Huh?"

Why couldn't this srell lift move any faster? "What happens with Mariella and myself is none of your business." I replied calmly.

The lift stopped, and I pushed through the doors, trying to leave Sakev behind. Sometimes, his immaturity was beyond baffling.

"Hey! Wait for me! So, you did get some time with her. I knew it! Good for you. I'm happy for you."

I stopped dead in my tracks. His voice had sounded sincere for those last four words, and that caught me by surprise.

He stopped a few steps later and looked back at me. "What?"

I smiled and shook my head. He was incorrigible, and immature, and a fool, but I could always count on him, even if he did like to make jokes at people's expense. "Nothing, you're just an unusual one, that's all."

"Well, yeah. That's what makes me unique. Oh, srell, I forgot to tell you. Vrehx wants to see you."

"I know, I'm heading to the launch bay now to meet him," I said as I started walking again.

"Will you have the energy after…the business with you and Mariella?" Sakev asked, waggling his eyebrows at me.

"Ketonsin idiot!" I snapped at him as Vrehx and the others looked at us, eyebrows raised. I waved Sakev off and marched over to Vrehx. "Sorry for the delay, sir. I was given bad information on where to find you."

Vrehx looked past me, shaking his head slightly. "I bet. Grab your gear, we leave in two minutes. Or do you have another vacation to go on?"

"No, sir. I'm here for this."

"Good. Two minutes." He turned away from me and finished getting his gear in order. Axtin winked at me and slung his pack onto his shoulders and boarded one of our two working shuttles. I could see Daxion already on board, double checking the instrument panel of the shuttle. *I guess he's flying us,* I thought as I went to the weapon's closet. My weapons had already been brought down and were sitting on a box near the shuttle, so all I needed was extra ammunition. I grabbed a few extra clips, an extra scope for my rifle, and a set of goggles.

I turned away from the weapons closet to see Vrehx with his finger in Sakev's face, undoubtedly telling him to get serious. Sakev smiled at him, said something, and boarded the shuttle. Vrehx looked over at me, frowned, and boarded as well. With a dejected sigh, I put the extra clips, scope, and goggles into my pack, grabbed my weapons, and boarded.

As the doors closed and Dax got the shuttle out of the hangar bay, the silence inside became deafening. I broke the silence by clearing my throat, then opened my mouth to speak.

Axtin beat me to it. "Was the trip worth it?"

"I'm sorry?" I asked.

He looked me straight in the face, his expression as serious as I've ever seen. "Was...the trip...worth it?"

"Yes, I believe it was. We found some information that Mariella, and Leena," I added in to emphasize my point, hoping he'd catch on to what the trip was about without me having to say it out loud, "might be able to use."

He nodded in understanding. "Good. Was it worth it in other ways?"

"Really?" I asked with a slight edge to my voice.

He smiled. "Guess Sakev mentioned the wager we had going?" The old Axtin was back. "Glad to have you back Tu'ver. Just, next time, let one of us know...we worry about you."

Sakev was trying not to laugh, and even Vrehx had a small grin.

I smiled. "Yes, *father.*" Sakev couldn't hold it in anymore. He burst out laughing, as did Axtin. Even Vrehx cracked a genuine smile.

He turned to me, letting the smile drop. "In all seriousness though, do not violate orders like that again. I know that you thought what you two were doing was important, but it was stupid and dangerous. We might have needed you here."

"Yes, sir. Again, my apologies for my actions."

"Don't apologize. I would have done the same in your situation." That surprised me. "Just don't do it again, that's all. Now, as to what we're doing here." He turned to face all of us, all of us getting serious and paying attention. "Can you hear me Dax?"

"Aye, sir," he said from up front.

"Good. We're on our way to Kangefi, a large island to the east of here. There are two Quake Stations on the island and the island is covered in jungle wetlands. While the lover here" nodding at me, "was out, another rift opened up and something came through."

"Any idea what it was?" I asked.

With a shake of the head, Vrehx answered. "No. Our sensors were affected by the energy of the rift. Karzin's team was out when it happened, and they think it was some sort of ship. It came in fast and hard. Rouhr is sending us as the first team in, Sk'lar's team is on stand-by until Karzin and his group get back in. Our mission is to find the ship, investigate, and try to determine if whatever, or whoever, is on board is friendly or not."

"And to make sure the Xathi don't get to it first," Axtin added in.

"Right," Vrehx acknowledged. He turned towards the front. "How long before we get there Daxion?"

"Ten minutes sir," was the answer.

Vrehx nodded. "Okay, load up, psych up…it's time to do our jobs."

I spent the next ten minutes checking my guns, making sure each was properly loaded and ready. My knife was strapped to my thigh, easy enough to snap out. I checked the scope on my rifle. It was broken. It must have broken in the rock slide and I just didn't notice. I quickly took it off, put the new scope on, and then strapped the goggles around my head. I turned them on, made sure they did what they were supposed to, then powered them down and lifted them up onto my forehead.

Axtin had his trusty hammer strapped to his back, as

well as the rest of the armory strapped to his waist, thighs, calves, arms, fingers, toes, hips, back, chest, arms, wrists, and probably even had some grenades and a missile launcher tucked away somewhere that I didn't want to think about. He was a walking arsenal and loved being that way. He firmly believed that he needed to have a weapon for every occasion, even if that occasion was a trip to the mess hall for breakfast.

Sakev and Vrehx, while different in personality, were similar in their weapon choices. Each carried two knives, two blasters, and a strap of grenades around their chest. The only real difference was that Sakev was our explosives expert, so he also carried a hip bag of explosives and detonators.

After Sakev got his gear in order, he quickly double checked Daxion's gear—a massive automatic rifle, a massive double-barreled rifle with a kick-back that even Axtin didn't want to play with, his three blasters, two knives, and his sword. Daxion was almost as proud of his sword as Axtin was of his hammer.

"We're here." Daxion called out.

We all looked at the screen Vrehx had out and saw the ship that had crashed. It was huge, bigger than the *Vengeance*, and sleeker looking as well. While the *Vengeance* had the bristling look of a warship, this thing looked like it had been built for luxury. It was long, sleek, and I couldn't see any weapons on it. There were some markings on the side of the ship - what I thought could be the name and registry but couldn't know for sure since the markings were unintelligible.

"Odd looking thing," Axtin said. We all nodded in agreement.

"Set us down close by, Daxion," Vrehx ordered. With a grunt of acknowledgement, Dax did as ordered. He landed the shuttle, and we all exited, weapons at the ready. Upon closer inspection of the outside, we could see some defensive weapons, but there weren't many, and these seemed to be small fire cannons, not something you'd use against a warship like the *Vengeance*.

"Be wary," Vrehx said. "Tu'ver, lead the way. Axtin behind. Dax and Sakev, bring up the rear."

I lead the way towards the ship. The damage it had caused to the jungle was substantial, and eerily similar to what we had done to the forest when we crashed. There were still small fires burning here and there, most of the trees had been snapped and destroyed, while a few still stood, as if they had bent to the ship and popped back up.

There were some dead animals here and there, and the ground had been torn up. Scorch marks around the engines of the ship were evident, but we couldn't tell if they were from the trip through the rift, coming into the atmosphere, or enemy fire.

"This doesn't seem right. Where is everyone? They crashed over an hour ago, and there's no one outside yet?" Axtin had a good point. It did seem odd.

"I'm not sure. Keep your head on straight though, don't get soft," Vrehx whispered back. We circled the ship, looking at everything, trying to find some way in. There were several holes all over the ship, with power cables sparking and popping from nearly all of them. Finally, I found an entrance that didn't have an obstruction, and at Vrehx's nod, I entered.

This ship was odd. The outer walls weren't very thick. It definitely wasn't built for defense. As a matter of fact, it looked like every place there was supposed to be a defensive weapon, and there weren't many of those, it was if a room had been built for the weapon. The interior of the ship, while not in good condition now, looked as if it was once beautiful, at least in this section.

"All clear," I announced to the others. The hole in the ship we used was in what appeared to be a leisure room. Couches, chairs, and small tables littered the area, with dozens of tiny fountains and hundreds of plants strewn everywhere.

A computer terminal sat in the corner, the screen blinking on and off. A glass wall to my left showed a room full of massage beds and stretching machines. To the right was a partially open door, flickering light coming through every few seconds or so.

"Does anyone else notice the distinct lack of life on this thing, or is that just me?" Sakev asked no one in particular.

I looked at Sakev and then all around. He was right, the only life in the room were the plants and us.

"Tu'ver, see if you can get anything from that terminal. Sakev and Dax, head left, report anything unusual. Or, anything at all. Axtin, you and I are heading through the door on the far wall to do the same."

It only took seconds to realized that even though the terminal link was still strong, the files were a jumble.

"I can't decipher their organizational structure, sir." I reported as I disconnected. "I'm sure I can crack it in time."

Vrehx shook his head. "Go with Axtin. Right now, our top priority is determining any immediate threats."

Axtin and I went to the right as ordered. Axtin, his weapons ready, waited as I pulled the door open and got out of the way. He entered first, me right behind. Our weapons weren't needed.

For the next three hours, we searched the ship as much as we could. There were only a few rooms we couldn't enter, but we returned with the same information as Sakev and Dax…it was empty.

There was nothing alive on the ship except us and plants. The problem was that there weren't any bodies. There was nothing. The ship was empty.

"The computer was a dead end as well," Vrehx told us after we reported back. "I couldn't find anything on there that our system was able to translate."

"What now?" I asked.

"We head back to the *Vengeance* and talk to the others. Try to figure this out. Let's move."

It was a quiet trip back home, each of us trying to figure out the mystery of the ship. The only thing we knew about it was the name that we had given it. Or more accurately, that Axtin had begun calling it.

The *Aurora*.

MARIELLA

I'd been pacing for hours. I refused to sit still. If I did, my fears would consume me. Leena and Jeneva tried in vain to distract me but I could tell they were both concerned as well.

Jeneva kept checking surveillance equipment hoping for more information.

Leena pretended she wasn't worried. She had faith in Axtin's ability to stay alive against a hostile enemy, we all did. But I could tell she was anxious by her distracted air.

It was sweet, in a way. I was glad to see that Leena found someone to care about so deeply.

But that didn't change the fact that something had dropped out of the sky, and no one knew what it was.

The doors to the docking bay abruptly opened and

the members of various strike teams strode in. No one looked injured, but I still held my breath. When strike team one entered the room, I dashed forward before I realized what I was doing.

"Tu'ver," my voice broke on his name as I collided with his solid chest and locked my arms around his waist. "I was so worried."

He encircled me in his arms, one hand around my waist and the other cupping the back of my head.

"It's all right. I'm fine," he said in a soothing tone, quiet enough so only I could hear him.

"Look at that," I heard someone, Sakev I think, say behind us. "Tu'ver found a human woman to tolerate him." There was a small ripple of laughter, quickly silenced by one stern look from Tu'ver.

I grinned against his chest, then I met Leena's surprised gaze. With everything going on, I never got the chance to tell her about me and Tu'ver.

Whoops.

"What did you find?" I asked, looking up at Tu'ver. I'd deal with the fallout with Leena later.

"A ship like nothing I've ever seen before," Tu'ver replied. I swear there was a touch of admiration in his voice. "But completely abandoned."

"There weren't any..." I couldn't bring myself to say the word *bodies.* Tu'ver shook his head, perplexed.

"We have a mystery on our hands, it seems," Vrehx

said, drawing everyone's attention. "Perhaps you three could lend your skills."

"Us?" Jeneva said, sounding excited as she stepped closer to Vrehx. He smiled warmly at her.

"Yes. The ship is quite large. It would take ages to do a thorough search. Jeneva, I'd like you to use your empathic abilities to sense survivors. The odds are low, but I'd like to be sure," Vrehx explained.

"Yes, sir," Jeneva grinned giving Vrehx a sassy little salute. Vrehx chuckled and shook his head before turning to my sister.

"Leena, I'd like you to gather samples of anything you think can be analyzed in the lab," he instructed. Leena replied with only a curt nod. Then Vrehx turned to me.

"Mariella," he said. "Tu'ver tells me you're an expert at locating and retrieving lost information."

"Oh," I replied, a deep blush coloring my cheeks. I don't know why I felt bashful all of a sudden. I was excellent at my job, but the thought of Tu'ver singing my praises made me giddy. "Yes, that's right."

"I'd like you to locate the ships logs. If anyone would find something relevant or be able to make sense of their language it would be you. See if you can find anything useful that might tell us who those people were and what happened to them," Vrehx said.

"I can do that," I grinned. Tu'ver gave my arm a light squeeze.

"We can't read anything on that ship, so a lot of this is going to be intuition. But Tu'ver says you're an archivist by trade and that tells me that you have an adaptable intellect to spot things others may miss," he continued as I blushed.

"I've done a fair amount of detective work," I replied. "I'll try to be helpful."

"Excellent," Vrehx nodded. "I'll give you three some time to gather whatever you think you'll need. Meet in the docking bay as soon as possible. No more than half an hour till we head back to *Aurora*."

"How do we know that's the name?" I asked.

"We don't," Axtin said with a grin. "But it came from the heavens and it seemed fitting."

"It may have come from the heavens, but that doesn't mean it won't bring demons of air and darkness with it," Vrehx said glumly. Each of us ruminated on that cheerful thought for a moment before he continued. "We sound like we have a plan. Let us go execute it so that we may all return safe."

"Yes, sir," Jeneva, Leena and I said in unison before hurrying away to prepare. Jeneva and I followed Leena to help her get her things together, since Jeneva didn't need anything and I already had a few blank data disks on me.

"When did you and Tu'ver get so friendly?" Leena asked when we were out of earshot. Jeneva linked her arm through mine and flashed a conspiratorial grin.

"We've always been friendly," I said, giving a noncommittal shrug.

"Mari, you know what I mean," Leena sighed, rolling her eyes up to the ceiling.

"Things just sort of...clicked...in Glymna," I answered, struggling to find the right words without saying too much.

"He's dangerous, Mari," Leena pressed, unable to let it go.

"They're all dangerous," I countered. "Axtin included."

"Tu'ver's kill count is almost double Axtin's," Leena exclaimed. "Bet you didn't know that, hmm?"

I didn't know that. I never pressured Tu'ver to talk about what he did as a sniper. If he wanted to talk about it, he would talk about it. And I would listen.

But until then, I was happy to be a distraction for him, so he wouldn't have to always be thinking about the horrible things happening around us.

"Be happy for me, Leena," I said, my shoulders sagging in defeat. "He's good to me. He's looked after me since the moment we were brought onto the *Vengeance*. Maybe you don't trust him completely. That's fine, I guess. But can you at least trust me?"

When Leena didn't immediately answer, Jeneva piped up.

"I think it's great!" She said with a big, if not slightly forced, smile. "If someone like you can warm up Tu'ver, then clearly he must have some redeeming qualities. That didn't come out right at all, did it?" She laughed nervously.

"I know what you meant," I said with a smile. The three of us walked into the lab. Leena immediately began digging through drawers and cabinets for anything she might need.

"The bioscanner is a bit cumbersome but it'll pick up on even the smallest amount of organic matter," she said, mostly to herself. She looked over her shoulder at me and Jeneva. "Do you think I'll need it?"

"I have no idea what you're talking about," Jeneva grinned. I couldn't help but laugh.

Suddenly, Leena sighed and set down her bag of equipment with an unceremonious thump.

"I always do that, don't I?" She asked, pressing her fingertips to the top of her nose bridge.

"Ask us about complicated equipment we know nothing about?" I ventured. "Yes, you do."

"No," Leena said. "I mean I tear you down whenever you feel happy about something."

"Oh," I said quietly, unsure of what else to say. The years we spent apart had damaged our relationship as sisters. For me, it was easy to forgive and forget but I knew that wasn't the case with Leena.

"I don't know what's wrong with me," Leena whispered.

"There's nothing wrong with you!" I protested. I closed the distance between us and gripped her shoulders. "That's crazy of you to say, and you know it."

"I've done such a shit job of being a big sister," Leena said. "I've been given a chance to do better and I'm just as bitchy as I was before."

"That's because you *are* a bitch, Leena," I sighed.

"Excuse me?" Leena's brows shot up, all apology vanishing from her face.

"You're a hardworking, brilliant, badass bitch who would go to the ends of the earth for the people you love," I continued. "If you weren't who you are, I couldn't be who I am."

"Is that why you're a ray of damn sunshine all the time? Because I'm a bitch?" Leena sputtered.

"You've finally figured it out," I sighed. "We're two halves of a whole. That's what sisters *are.*"

"I feel like I got the short end of the stick in this situation," Leena said.

"Yes, you did. That's your burden as a big sister," I teased.

"I am so confused right now," Jeneva said, looking back and forth between Leena and me.

"I want to be the little sister!" Leena whined playfully. "Why can't we take turns being the bitch?"

"Because you're way too good at it," I laughed.

"Is this how normal sisters communicate?" Jeneva asked.

"Pretty much," Leena shrugged. She pulled me in for a hug. I squeezed her back. "If Tu'ver makes you happy, then I'm happy for you." She said into my ear.

"Thank you," I said, letting the hug go on for a moment longer before letting go.

"So, if I call Amira a bitch she'll forgive me?" Jeneva asked, skeptically.

"Oh, definitely not," I giggled into my palm. "As the little sister, I can get away with it. The older sister can't."

"This makes no fucking sense," Jeneva covered her eyes with her hands and groaned.

"Families don't make sense," Leena added. "You should hear the arguments Calixta comes up with."

"She gets more like you every day," I smiled. "You're in for a rough ride when she becomes a teenager."

"I'm trying not to think about it," Leena smirked as she slung her equipment bag over her shoulder.

The three of us walked side by side, arms linked. The more time we spent on the *Vengeance,* the more Jeneva felt like a third sister.

"So," Leena said after a moment of silence. "Did you and Tu'ver...?"

"What?" I asked, looking at the ground. I could feel a blush coloring my cheeks. I knew what Leena was going to ask. I was more than happy to play dumb, though I knew it wouldn't deter her.

"Did you fuck?" Jeneva asked. I almost tripped over myself. Leena threw her head back, cackling.

"Jeneva!" I gasped as my shock gave way to laughter.

"Well, Leena didn't feel like being her usual blunt self, so I thought I'd do it for her," Jeneva shrugged.

"How thoughtful of you," Leena smirked. She turned her attention back to me. "But, seriously, did you?"

"Yes," I said hesitantly, unable to stop the massive smile that spread across my face when I thought back to that moment in the valley. Jeneva and Leena squealed with laughter.

"Tell me everything!" Leena demanded. "You have to! I'm your sister."

"Tell me everything because I'm nosy," Jeneva added.

"You're both completely ridiculous," I said, ducking my head as if I could escape them.

"He's so quiet all the time, I bet he's a dirty talker in the bedroom," Jeneva speculated.

"Is he big?" Leena asked, wide eyed.

"If this is your way of making an effort to accept my

relationship, then I'd rather you just go back to being a bitch," I said, trying to subdue my own laughter.

"He's big," Leena nodded as if I'd confirmed everything. They were still howling, and I was still blushing when we entered the docking bay.

"What's going on here?" Axtin said, a mischievous gleam in his eye as he looked at Leena.

"Oh, nothing you need to worry about," Leena said, breezing past him to stow her things in the carrier.

"You human females are so strange," Vrehx said, shaking his head as Jeneva took her place beside him.

"Yeah, but it makes things interesting. Wouldn't you agree?" Jeneva replied.

"Interesting is one way to put it," Vrehx said with a nod.

Tu'ver said nothing. He only looked at me, with one brow slightly raised.

"You don't want to know," I said as I walked past him and climbed into the carrier.

I was the only one who saw the corner of his mouth twitch up into a smile.

TU'VER

The eight of us flew back to the *Aurora* crash site, hoping that the Xathi hadn't yet made it there. The trip didn't take long as we explained to the women what the ship looked like inside and out. Leena was particularly interested in the plants as they might give her an idea of what sort of environment they'd originally evolved in. Any sort of new problem seemed to excite her.

I glanced at the excitement on Mariella's face as they whispered between them about possibilities. The sisters were more alike than one might suppose at first glance.

Dax flew us in a widening spiral pattern around the ship, trying to do an aerial recon of the area. We didn't see anything, so Vrehx gave the order to land. As Dax was setting the shuttle down on the uneven ground, the women were bumped around due to the rough landing. Mariella and Jeneva both let out a small yelp, making the rest of us chuckle a bit.

I flashed Mariella an apologetic smile when she glared at me, and her answering grin warmed me.

"Just because we didn't see anything the first time, let's not take this lightly," Vrehx said as we all stood, ready to exit the shuttle. "Tu'ver and Axtin first, myself and Sakev come out next. Daxion escorts the women once we've given the 'all-clear.' Understood?"

Vrehx was right, it was better to be cautious. We all nodded, and Vrehx gave us the go-ahead to move out. Axtin and I led the way, weapons up. I couldn't see anything, except what we had seen before—the destructive path of the *Aurora's* crash and the *Aurora* herself.

Vrehx and Sakev came out next and we formed a protective circle around the shuttle door. Dax and the women followed us out a few seconds later, and everything was clear. The *Aurora* was maybe a hundred yards away, and the fires that were burning when we were here a few hours ago were now smoldering heaps, leaving thick patches of smoke in the air.

As we made our way towards the ship, we heard voices coming from our left. We stopped, weapons ready but pointed towards the ground. Out of the jungle came a group of humans, and as we stood there, the group continued to grow. When the group finally stopped coming out of the trees they numbered close to forty, although I was certain more stay hidden in the trees.

They kept walking towards us, finally stopping about ten to twelve yards away from us. They were a ragged bunch, not in dress or looks, but in behavior. They seemed nervous, anxious, and angry. They were dressed fairly well, at least as well as most of the people were dressed in Glymna, and they were clean. They just seemed...different.

"What are you *things* doing here?" one of the men asked. I could taste the venom in his voice, that's how much emphasis he put into it. He was a tall man with dark skin, long black hair, and a slight limp to his left leg. I wasn't sure if it was due to an injury or if that leg was shorter than his right because when he stood, he seemed to stand with his right leg slightly bent.

Vrehx stepped forward, pointedly not holstering his weapon as he did. Not threatening, but not backing down either. "We're here to investigate this ship, that's all. We'd appreciate some help if you were willing."

They didn't look happy to see us, but if we showed that we're willing to work with them, maybe we could start some peaceful dialogue.

Then the other man spoke and ruined the idea. "You

want us to work with *you*? Why would we ever work with alien filth like you?"

Jeneva stepped forward before Vrehx could say anything. "What the hell is wrong with you? Vrehx and his people are trying to *help* us, not hurt us. They're fighting against the Xathi," her voice crackled with anger. "They're not the problem here."

"All aliens are the same! It's their fault that we're hurting, their fault that we've each lost family or friends, THEIR FAULT that my daughter is permanently paralyzed! The only good alien on this world is a dead alien!"

Spittle flew from his mouth and several of the people clustered behind him spoke up, agreeing with their leader. They were poorly armed with knives, pipes, clubs, and a few hand-blasters, but they did outnumber us, and a fight could end up with some of us hurt or dead.

Axtin and Daxion took a step forward, putting themselves between the group and the women. Sakev and I stepped a bit off to the side, making sure we had open sight lines...just in case.

A quick glance at Mariella showed me that she was nervous, maybe a bit scared. This confrontation bothered her. Therefore, it bothered me. I fingered my knives. This needed to end quickly.

"We were aliens when we landed on this planet, and

on every other planet we've ever landed on. Does that mean we should die too?" Jeneva didn't back down.

Vrehx lightly touched Jeneva's shoulder and whispered something to her. She nodded, reluctantly I could tell, and stepped back.

"See? See?!" the man yelled out. "You even follow their orders! I bet you're screwing the bastard, aren't you, you whore?"

That was the wrong thing to say. Vrehx barely caught Jeneva as she jumped forward, spewing curses and threats that made me go wide-eyed. Vrehx said something to Axtin and Dax and they both grunted as they stepped forward.

"No weapons!" Vrehx commanded. "Disable only!"

Disable meant that we couldn't use our swords, or axes, not to mention blaster rifles. What we did have were sonic shockers - specifically for dealing with unruly humans. Rouhr had commanded that all personnel traveling outside the Vengeance carry a shocker, which looked like a miniature blaster carry the weapons to protect ourselves after Axtin's encounter with them in Duvest.

Within seconds Axtin and Dax had switched from their weapons to the sonics. The high-pitched whine coming from the devices shredding my nerves, even pointed away from us.

There we stood, pointing sonic weapons at the

humans, who had no idea that they weren't blaster rifles.

They did the most practical thing in that situation.

The humans at the back of the group took off running, the rest of them following a bit slower, but not by much. The leader of the group stood firm, for an impressive ten or eleven seconds before realizing he was alone. Then he turned and ran off, yelling curses at us as he did.

Dax turned off his gun, the whine dissipating quickly. As soon as we were able to hear one another again, Leena was the first voice to be heard. "What in the holy hell was that all about? Who was that moron?"

Axtin laughed as he slapped her behind. "There's always an idiot and their followers everywhere. He's just another one." She promptly slapped him back, in the face, drawing a look of shock from Axtin and a burst of laughter from the rest of us.

"Don't you slap me in the butt again, you got it muscle-boy?" While the slap had force behind it, her voice didn't, it was almost playful.

She seemed to have been researching more Valorni mating rituals.

That would be exciting for the rest of us.

"Enough. We've got enough going on without having the two of you playing around." Vrehx was not happy.

I went Mariella's side. "You okay?" I asked quietly.

She looked up at me, her eyes telling me the whole story before her words did. "No. That group wanted to hurt us. They hated you, all of you. All of us. I can't believe how much anger they had."

"I know. It takes time for different races to come together. The K'ver and Valorni and Skotans all hated one another, and even though there were several cease fires, we couldn't come together to actually establish peace until the Xathi arrived."

"Hey, you two...get over here," Axtin's booming voice interrupted us. We walked over to the others as Vrehx tried to calm Jeneva down.

"Let them be, Jeneva. Not everyone is going to like us, no matter how much proof is in front of them," he was trying to keep his voice calm for her.

"Did you not hear what they called me, what they said about you? They're idiots. They deserve to get their asses kicked from one side of the planet to the other."

"Will you calm down?" Oh, that was a mistake. Jeneva's face went red as she stared at Vrehx. I had never seen him back down from anything, ever...but he backed down now. That look on her face made all of us, the males anyway, take a step back.

I ventured into the danger-zone and risked opening

my mouth. "Did anyone notice that was a larger group than normal?"

"Well, other than the mob in Duvest that followed me around…yeah, that was a bigger group of hatefuls than before," Axtin answered.

"Eh, so what? Just call in our mountains here to scare them off, no big deal," Leena chimed in, indicating me and Dax.

"No big deal?" Mariella shot back. "Are you kidding? This group might have been scared off, but what if it's a bigger group? What if they have better weapons? What if they just decide to shoot instead of talk?"

Before any of the others could say anything, I broke in. "She has a bit of a point. I've heard all your stories, and luckily, we didn't have an issue in Glymna, but this was a sizeable group. There were more of them in the trees as well. This could eventually become a problem for us."

Leena and Jeneva both started to say something, but Vrehx put up his hand to stay them. "Enough. Our mission right now is to investigate the ship. The human problem isn't going to go away any time soon. We can solve it when we're back on the *Vengeance*."

His words made sense, but my gut told me we'd be dealing with the 'human problem' sooner than we wanted.

MARIELLA

Mariella

"You know, the name *Aurora* suits her," I said to Tu'ver, tilting my head as far back as I could to look at the gleaming hull. "She's beautiful." I could only imagine what it looked like soaring between the stars.

"It means rebirth to the Valorni," Tu'ver said. "Does it mean something in your language?"

"It means dawn," I replied. "But I found a book a few years ago about natural phenomena on Earth. There was something called aurora borealis that only happened in the far north. It looked like rivers of light in the sky."

"That doesn't happen here?" Tu'ver asked.

"Not that I've ever seen," I said sadly. "I would have liked to see it back on Earth."

"It's a shame," Tu'ver agreed. We fell in line with the others.

Inside the ship, Vrehx showed Leena his initial scans of the ship's interior in an attempt to figure out the best place for Leena to search for samples.

Jeneva stood a few yards away from everyone else, her eyes squeezed shut in concentration.

"Any chance of survivors?" I said softly to Vrehx, nodding my head in Jeneva's direction.

"It doesn't look like it," Vrehx answered, his mouth tight with concern. I watched Jeneva. Her brow was deeply furrowed, her lips turning pale.

"She's over-exerting herself." Vrehx quickly strode over to her and touched her shoulder gently. Her eyes fluttered open as she sucked in a deep breath. Vrehx supported Jeneva as he led her back to the group.

"Did you feel anything?" Leena asked.

"I'm not sure," Jeneva said. Her voice was breathless. A light sheen of sweat had broken out on her forehead.

"What do you mean?" Vrehx asked gently.

"Sometimes, I thought I felt *something*," Jeneva said hesitantly as if she couldn't think of the right words. "Not like a person, but something else.

"Is it possible for her to pick up on the emotions of

animals?" Leena asked Vrehx. Vrehx rubbed his chin as he considered the possibility.

"If it were a particularly intelligent species, it's possible," Vrehx said after a pause.

"It didn't feel like that," Jeneva insisted. "The most intelligent native creatures on this planet are the damn trees."

"Then what did it feel like?" Axtin pressed.

"I don't know!" Jeneva exclaimed in frustration. "All I know is that I felt something, and it didn't feel right."

"Tu'ver, I want you to find a good perch and guard the perimeter," Vrehx instructed. "If any of the hostile humans are planning something, put them down before they even get the chance."

Tu'ver nodded once. Sometimes, I forgot how dangerous Tu'ver really was. But he was a trained killer. The best of the best, apparently.

"I'd prefer it if you accompanied me," Tu'ver said to me.

"I have my own orders to follow," I replied. "I have to figure out what happened to the poor people who were on this ship." The longer I spent on this ghost vessel, the more it bothered me. I didn't want to figure it out because Vrehx asked me to. I wanted to figure it out for myself. And for them. Whoever they were.

"I'll tell Vrehx I'm going to guard you," Tu'ver said.

I reached for his arm before he could walk away.

"I work better if I'm allowed to survey a space alone," I said gently. "It helps me get into the mindset of what I'm studying. Besides, Vrehx is asking you to protect everyone, not just me. I think that's more important."

"Mariella," Tu'ver said, a touch of warning in his voice. "This place could be dangerous. There could be traps or hostiles waiting to ambush us."

"Jeneva would have sensed them," I pointed out.

"Would she? She's only just beginning to understand her abilities," Tu'ver countered.

"Tu'ver," I replied. "Trust me, please? I'll have my commlink on me the whole time. I'll keep my location updated. I'll be fine." I knew he didn't want to agree. I could practically see arguments forming in his mind.

"All right," he agreed, much to my surprise. "Check in often. Don't take risks." He gave my hand a light squeeze before striding back towards the shuttle outside.

On the far side of the room was a set of double doors. One door had practically been ripped from its hinges. The other was badly dented. It was likely the damage was sustained in the crash, but there was also a chance it wasn't. It looked more promising than anything else as far as I could tell.

I pulled up the rough schematic of the ship on my datapad and tried to orient myself. If I was right, and the map was accurate, that corridor would lead me deeper into the heart of the vessel.

After double checking that my location tracking was activated and my commlink worked, I forced my way through the doors.

"Be careful, Mari." Leena's voice came through my earpiece.

"You too. Stay in touch," I said. I turned right down the corridor, heading towards the slender nose of the vessel.

The walls were made of smooth metal, bare except for small signs in a language I didn't recognize. The whorls and symbols were like nothing I'd ever seen before. Most of the signs were posted outside of doorways that were sealed shut. I couldn't find anything that looked like it could open the doors. Perhaps they'd been motion activated before the crash.

"Not getting anything on my bioscanner," Leena's frustrated voice came after a few minutes. "It's almost like this ship has always been empty."

"Like it was launched without anyone inside?" Axtin replied.

"No way," came the drawling voice of Sakev. "A ship like this would go for billions in the Skota Capulus. No way would they just launch it into space."

"Unless this is just a really, *really* fancy space probe," Dax commented.

"Yeah, a space probe with crew cabins and zero protection against a hostile environment seems real likely," Axtin shot back.

"Minimize commlink chatter," Vrehx ordered.

I wasn't sure how long I wandered in silence, but eventually, I came to another set of damaged doors that looked promising. There was one thing that struck me as odd about the doors. They were mostly undamaged, except for indentations at the seam where the doors met. That sort of damage wasn't caused by the crash.

Someone had tried to pry the doors open.

"I may have found something," I said into the commlink. I put my hands where the indentations were and forced the doors open. The metal was lightweight. These doors were never designed to be a barricade. This ship never expected to be attacked, if that's what even happened.

"Report," came Vrehx's voice.

"Damage that seems unlikely to be caused by a crash," I replied. I pulled the flash beam I'd grabbed from the shuttle and shone it into the darkness. Light pooled over rows of desks and chairs. The tech on the desktop was foreign to me but the general layout of everything looked familiar. "I think I just found the control room."

"Standby," Vrehx announced. "I'll send someone to come assist you in getting things up and running."

"I can try," I replied to him, stepping into the dark room.

"I'm still sending someone," his gruff voice returned.

Not arguing further, I took a seat at the closest terminal. On the desk was an upright hollow square approximately eighteen inches wide and ten inches tall. There was no keyboard to speak of or anything else on the surface of the desk.

I ran a hand along the outside of the square, looking for a switch or a button. There was nothing. I was becoming acutely aware of the darkness pressing in around me. I pushed the chair closer to the desk as if it offered any sort of protection. My knee bumped the bottom of the desk. I must have hit something because suddenly a bright pale blue light filled the inside of the square.

"See," I said to myself. "Who needs a soldier?"

Black writing in the same swirling language I'd seen in the hallways appeared stark against the bright light. I reached toward one of the symbols, my hand passing right through the light. What I assumed was a file opened.

Though I couldn't understand any of the writing, I began to use my data pad to record the symbols.

I asked the computer to begin analysis of all known records and give me the closest match it could to assist in translating. It would take a while, however.

Till then, I had to rely on guesswork.

If I could figure out how to navigate between the different folders, the information would be there. From everything I'd noticed, humans had a very specific way they liked to organize these sorts of things. As did Skotans, K'ver, and Valorni. Remarkably, they were all quite similar.

I opened a folder, touching my finger to the light to open the first thing inside. Endless rows of text appeared that I couldn't decipher.

I figured out a way to navigate back to a section where the symbols looked familiar and touched my finger on another folder.

This one bore fruit.

"I found surveillance footage," I said, excitedly.

"Anything useful?" Vrehx replied. I watched the figures move across the light screen. They were bipedal, but the files must have been corrupted.

"I'm recording it on my datapad and interfacing it to the computer on the Vengeance to see if I can make any sense of it," I told Vrehx.

"Keep me apprised of any danger," he replied.

"Nothing looks out of the ordinary," I said, frowning. "Respectively, of course. They seem to be performing standard duties. No one appears to be panicked or distressed.

I began to transfer the entire folder onto my

datapad. The initial recordings were easy, but actual data transfer was a bit more difficult. I had learned a method a few years back just in case I ever worked with incompatible tech. I was glad it finally came in handy, although I wouldn't know if the files transferred correctly until I was back on the *Vengeance.*

I continued my methodical examination of the strange terminal. I opened another file in a new folder. A warbling noise came from a speaker I couldn't see, nearly scaring me out of my skin. At first, it sounded like static and commlink interference but as I listened, I noticed distinct vocal patterns. This was their language.

"I found audio logs too," I said into the comm.

"Excellent work, Mariella," Vrehx praised. "Any luck elsewhere, team?"

"Nothing the bioscanner recognizes as organic, but I took a few samples just in case," Leena reported back.

"No signs of life elsewhere," Axtin called in.

"Okay, everyone head back to the shuttle to regroup," Vrehx ordered.

I let the audio continue to play as I set up my datapad for another complicated ghost transfer. Suddenly, the voices became quicker and higher in pitch. There were other sounds too. Thumps, bangs, and the screech of metal on metal.

Then came an unmistakable scream. I shut the audio off quickly, my breath hitching in my throat. My heart fluttered in my chest as I tried to tell myself that I didn't know what that sound was. I wouldn't know until I was back on the *Vengeance* where I could properly translate it. Where it was safe.

I quickly transferred the audio file and fled the room, leaving the terminal glowing behind me. My skin felt prickly as I hurried down the corridor. After a few moments, I realized I'd gone the wrong way. I pulled up the schematic, worried that I'd discover I was hopelessly lost in this shadowy labyrinth.

According to my location tracking, I was farther from the center of the ship that I feared.

Dim light from further down the corridor gave me another option.

"I think I found another hole in the hull," I said into the comm. "I'll walk around the outside of the *Aurora* to get back to the shuttle." The thought of walking back through the dark, creaky spacecraft alone was enough to give me the shivers. I didn't like it here. I wasn't sure what the audiotapes would reveal, but I felt in my bones that something horrible had happened here.

"Tu'ver," I said quietly, not caring if the others heard.

"I'm here, Mari," he replied.

"Okay, good," I sighed. I felt better knowing he was listening as I stepped in and out of shadows black as pitch.

I hurried through the corridors as quickly as

possible. Some of the walkways were so badly damaged that I had to shimmy through sideways. I didn't realize I was holding my breath until the sunlight hit my face and I gulped down a lung full of fresh air.

I broke into a run as soon as my feet touched the forest floor and circumvented the ships massive girth. The others were already gathered at the shuttle waiting for me.

I didn't care that I was the straggler. I was just happy not to be alone in the belly of the ship. Next time Tu'ver offered to come with me when I worked, I wouldn't turn him down. I'd never hear the end of it, but it'd be worth it.

"Mariella!" Tu'ver called. I smiled, lifting my hand to wave when it dawned on me that he didn't sound excited.

It was a warning.

TU'VER

J ust as Mariella emerged from the breach in the
hull, the threat sprang from the forest.

Fast, faster than any human I'd seen.

In the half-second he had his hands on Mariella, I'd
begun to catalogue the differences.

I jumped in, grabbed him from behind around the
chest, and threw him away from her.

He rolled and tumbled clear, got back onto all fours,
and snarled at us.

The eyes were white, just…white. There was no iris,
or at least no color to the iris. And, as for his skin, it
was covered in a thin layer of crystal, some of which
had rubbed off onto my arms when I grabbed him.

I wiped my arms clean, motioned Mariella to get

back behind the others, and faced off with this feral human.

He charged me, snapping his jaws like an animal as he leapt in the air. I sidestepped him, bringing my fist down on his shoulder as he landed, then immediately followed with a kick to the knee. It didn't faze the creature as he rolled away from me and charged at me again. I let him get close, and as he leapt at me again, I started to fall back and flipped him over me.

I rolled to my feet, turned around, and ran over to where he was trying to get back up. He was in obvious pain as he seemed to have landed on a jagged stump of a tree that had been broken from the impact of the Aurora. He rolled over and I kicked him in the head.

As he staggered back, I unsheathed my knife and flipped it in my hand, laying the blade against my arm. He sluggishly gained his feet, snarled and snapped at me again, and I hit him in the side of the head with the hilt of my knife.

He dropped like a rock, his breathing shallow.

"Somebody tie this damn thing up," I said as I looked back at the others. Savek and Axtin came over as Daxion took some cable out of a pack.

I went up to Mariella, cupping her cheek in my hand. "Are you okay?"

She was still shaking, but she nodded. "What the fuck is wrong with him?"

I repressed a grin at her cursing and pulled her in close. "That is the product of Xathi 'science.' I believe," I said quietly. I looked back at it, now fully tied up. It had already regained consciousness and was snarling and biting at the others. "We need to figure out what happened to him exactly."

"Really? You want to *study* this thing? We should just kill it and dump it in the jungle somewhere," Axtin declared.

Daxion agreed. "My cousin is correct. We cannot leave it alive. What if it can somehow call for help?"

"Then we deal with it when that moment comes," I argued.

"Why do you think it's Xathi related?" Mariella asked me. She still shook; this creature was obviously bothering her.

Before I answered, I looked at the others. Vrehx whispered with Jeneva, who was holding her head and pointing at the creature. Leena observed it, taking pictures with her data pad.

Sakev stood off to the side, trying not to look at the thing. Axtin and Daxion were shuffling back and forth, trying to stay out of its reach as it tried to roll and worm-crawl its way around. Axtin kicked it again, bringing out another snarl.

"The crystals growing on its skin," I said matter-of-factly. "Unless this is some new kind of disease, virus, bacteria, or mutation that you ladies don't know about, it's the only thing that makes sense."

"Tu'ver is right." We all looked over to see Vrehx approaching. Jeneva walked away, still holding her head. "Sakev, go keep an eye on her please, just in case anything else comes around."

"Aye," Sakev said as he jogged over to Jeneva.

"As I was saying," Vrehx started, "I think Tu'ver's right. This most likely has something to do with the Xathi. However, I agree with Axtin and Dax, we need to kill it and move on."

"What? No!" Leena's head snapped up from her data pad and she looked at Vrehx. "We need to study this thing. If this is a new weapon used by the Xathi we need to know what happened to this poor man and why."

"And you're not wrong, but we don't have the time or the resources to deal with something like this."

"I disagree," I said as I took a step forward. "There's an unused Quake Station a few miles from here. We can hold him there and observe him."

Vrehx shook his head. "We don't know what it is, and if it does have something to do with the Xathi, it's too dangerous. We kill it, dump it, and get back to the *Vengeance*."

"With all due respect, sir. You're wrong on this." Everyone looked at me with wide eyes. "If this is Xathi related, then that's precisely why we *should* study it. If this is something that is their doing, we need to know so we know how to combat it."

"Why are you so adamant about doing this?" Axtin asked.

"Because, I've seen something like this before on my home world, heard rumors of experiments," I said darkly, as I remembered back. "What if they're trying something similar here?"

"I had no idea. How bad was it?" I looked at Axtin as he asked. He was just curious, and I didn't blame him, but it was a hard question to answer.

"Very bad. Let's just leave it at that." I turned to Vrehx and looked him square in the face. "I'm not trying to undermine your authority, I'm really not. But, we need to know what is happening, or we're going to be ill-prepared for when things *do* happen."

He stared at me for a several heartbeats. I wasn't sure if he was trying to make me back down or not, but I didn't move. I didn't change my facial expression, I barely even blinked.

Vrehx was wrong on this one, and he needed to know it.

"If you two don't mind me interrupting your little staring contest," Jeneva walked back, waving off Vrehx's look of concern. "It's fine. Since he's unconscious, I can handle it." She flashed me a smile as she kept talking.

"I've seen creatures in the water mutate over the course of a few months because one of the spiders pissed in it. I've seen walking trees eat people. But I have never in my life seen anything like that man. So…regardless of what you think, darling dear," she said in an arch voice as she put her hand on Vrehx's arm. "Tu'ver and Leena are right. We need to know what is happening with him."

Out of the corner of my eye, I watched Axtin and Sakev both turn around to hide their faces. Daxion just pursed his lips and turned to look at the creature.

Not one to lose an advantage, I pressed my point. "The better we know our enemy, the better we defeat them. We can take shifts watching it at the Quake Station, keep it away from the ship and the others just in case. You know it's the right decision."

Vrehx's eyes flashed in anger as he stared back at me. "Don't push your luck. Not now." He took a deep breath and looked between Jeneva, Leena, and me. "Fine. We take it to the station and watch it in eight-hour shifts. And," he smiled grimly, "Your idea, your job. You get to have the first shift."

I returned his smile. "As you command."

None of them knew the depths of the Xathi evil.

I'd happily watch to make sure it didn't catch us unawares.

MARIELLA

Mariella

"Mari, stop pacing. You're going to make me sick," Leena snapped, looking up from her datapad. She'd been analyzing the samples she took from the *Aurora* since we got back. I hadn't been able to make much progress in translating the audio logs.

Two days had passed since we left the *Aurora*. Tu'ver and the others were still at the Quake station monitoring the deranged human. As I understood it, they were taking shifts a few days at a time. Dax was here now, on the *Vengeance*, but he was going back to the Quake station in the morning to give someone else a break. I selfishly hoped it would be Tu'ver.

As soon as I'd reluctantly climbed into the shuttle,

leaving Tu'ver behind to deal with that person, I logged into the *Vengeance* computers tied to the library to see if the software had finished its analysis of the images and data I had sent it. The computer was going to look through all its records to see if there was any clue that would lead me to be able to translate. However, the thought of sitting and working and sifting through endless amounts of data was more unappealing than it had ever been in my life.

"I can't help it!" I whined, hating that I sounded like a five-year-old child and unable to stop myself. "I feel like I'm going to jump out of my skin. How can you be so calm?"

"I'm not," Leena replied. "I'm incredibly anxious knowing that people I care about are alone on some dilapidated Quake station a stone's throw from a mysterious spacecraft crash, in an area full of anti-alien hostiles, and apparently, victims of psychological Xathi warfare."

"How are you not a mess like I am?" I asked.

"Take your emotions out of the equation," Leena suggested. "I know it's hard for you. But this is how I'm thinking about it. Axtin is perfectly capable of handling himself should anything attack the Quake station. I also know that I can be helpful by getting these samples analyzed."

"Are you telling me to go be useful somewhere?" I asked wryly.

"Yes," Leena replied. "You've been useless since we got back."

"Thanks a lot," I snarked.

"It's the truth. And if there's anything you can count on me for, it's the truth," Leena shrugged. "Go to the library and get some work done. I promise you'll feel better." She gave me an encouraging smile.

"You're right," I sighed, scooping up the datapad I'd been pretending to look at while I loitered in the lab.

"I'm always right," Leena replied.

"And so humble," I tossed over my shoulder as I left the lab.

In the library, the modified computer terminal had indeed finished running the myriad of comparative algorithm programs I had in my arsenal.

There were nearly a hundred different potential matches, but each was quickly ruled out due to inconsistencies in various aspects of the data I had recorded.

As I went through the list, I wondered at the near impossibility of the task. Attempting to translate something based on pictures of symbols with no other reference was daunting on the best days.

Alright. The real word for that was impossible.

Until the computer gave me a lifeline.

Records indicated that at some point in their history, the Valorni had contacted a race of nomadic traders known as the Otra. They'd sold waste management technology acquired from yet another race that contained the same markings.

As luck would have it, the waste management technological upgrades had come with extensive written instructions that the Otra had translated into High Valorni for the customers.

It was a thin, weak link, but right now I didn't have anything else.

Using the technical manual, which thanks to the Skotans obsession with record keeping had been digitized, as a cross reference, I was able to finally get a rough translation.

The result was a bunch of choppy sentence fragments sprinkled with misplaced verbs and adjectives. Not perfect, but I'd worked with less before.

It took a few hours for me to find all the words that were incorrectly translated and replace them with more probable words but I eventually I had a complete translation that was at least eighty-five percent accurate.

I also found the name of the ship. It was, *She Who Glides in The Night*.

Not quite *Aurora*. I took a second to feel bad for Axtin. I liked his name better. Then I got back to work.

Leena was right. Work was a fantastic distraction. The deeper I let myself fall into translating the texts, the less frantic I felt about Tu'ver.

He'd be proud of me if he knew how much I'd accomplished. The thought made me a little bit giddy.

I was hopeless.

The next step of the process was to set up a phonetic translation program. Since none of the programs at my disposal had ever encountered this language, I had to set the links between words, groups of words, and phrases to the human equivalent in order to give them sounds.

Luckily the Otra had supplied a few lines of this themselves, which the Valorni had translated into their language.

I spent another several hours reverse engineering this to make links between written words and their human counterparts using Valorni vocabulary as the bridge.

It was incredibly likely that the audio logs contained far more individual words and sounds than I'd been able to translate from the written words, but the computer program should be able to give me a rough translation that I would need to smooth out.

In the interest of research about an unknown species, I wanted to translate every single audio file, but the amount of time and power that would require would be immense. Though we had located a stable power source some weeks ago, General Rouhr still advised us to be conservative with our power usage just in case anything should happen.

I quickly used the recently translated texts to look for audio files timestamped close to the date of the crash.

It was then that I found something strange.

There were no audio logs the day of the crash.

Or the day before.

The last audio log was time stamped a full week before the *Aurora* fell through the rift. The video files I transferred stopped eight days before the crash.

Curious, I opened the last audio file. It didn't transfer properly. It looked as if there were a filmy substance over the camera lenses, blurring the images. The footage itself was jerky, sometimes repetitive.

But even then, nothing looked particularly out of the ordinary. I couldn't get a clear look at these beings. They walked on two legs, dressed primarily in dark colors suggesting some sort of uniform, and moved from place to place at a leisurely stroll or a brisk walk. I saw nothing that suggested an attack of any kind.

Frustrated, I returned to the audio logs. From the translated file titles, I determined that about half of the logs were routine documentation of the *Aurora's* day-to-day operations and the other half were personal logs.

I decided to start with the personal logs. A female who was registered as a service crewmember had recorded almost twice as many as anyone else. From the translated text, I could see her name would have been very similar to Adastria.

The stiff voice generated by the computer filled the small library, the words still jerky and awkward, but the meaning intelligible.

"The wealthy man from the upper level asked me to come by his room tonight. I think I will. He looks like he could be fun."

It stopped there. I moved onto the next.

"He was sweeter than I thought he'd be. He had food and drinks ready when I arrived. We didn't even do anything at first. We just sat and talked for hours. I don't want to jump to conclusions, but I think he might be something special."

The next log wasn't recorded until a few days later.

"I spoke too soon. He started acting strange. He told me he couldn't see me anymore. He said he needed to listen to what the Queen says. I have no idea what that could possibly mean. He probably met someone else. I bet this was all a game to him." Adastria made a sound that was like a sniffle. *Perhaps she'd been crying when she recorded this. Well, whatever her species did that was like crying.*

I felt bad for her, this strange woman I'd never meet.

"The head serviceman said something odd when he was giving out our assignments today. Instead of giving me a task list, he simply told me to do what the Queen asks. Who is this Queen people keep talking about? She must be an important guest."

It was strange. Maybe her people had her a monarchy?

I skipped down the next log, recorded next day.

"The Queen is going to take care of us all. We can live forever if we do what she says. I'm not sure I believe it, but whenever I think about it my chest feels light and wonderful. I should listen to the Queen."

I was more perplexed than ever.

"Something isn't right. People have started doing terrible things for the Queen. I saw a man tackle a sanitation crewmember and rip her hair right out of her scalp. Why would the Queen want us to do things like that? Something is wrong."

The horrible realization struck me just before I played the next log. The Xathi had queens capable of influencing the mind of a weaker species. Tu'ver's own people had been subjected to such horrors.

The monotone automated voice of the translation program made hearing it all the more haunting. I wished Tu'ver was here. I'd like to hear his thoughts on all of this and I didn't fancy sitting in a dimly lit room by myself anymore.

"The Queen demands blood. I don't want to do anything bad but she's going to make me. I can feel her claws scraping inside my skull. She won't leave me alone. Please, please just leave me alone."

Tears welled in my eyes as I opened the last audio log. I wasn't sure I could bear any more.

"I have to go open the airlocks now. The Queen is going to let us swim in the stars," The automated voice said.

"No, no, no," I whispered, lifting my hands to cover my mouth. There were a few moments of silence before the deafening sound of whooshing air blew through the speakers. Then came the screams.

The last thing I heard before the audio logs stopped completely was the same cryptic phrase over and over.

"The Queen commands it. The Queen commands it. The Queen commands it."

I shut off the audio before the clip finished.

I had to tell General Rouhr.

I don't fully remember walking from the library to his office. My mind was numb as it replayed what I'd heard on the logs.

When I reached General Rouhr's office, I didn't speak right away. He was sitting at his desk, bent over his console. He looked up, blinking in surprise when he saw me.

"Mariella, you're looking pale. Are you well?" General Rouhr asked, his concern genuine. Too nauseous to speak, I placed the datapad containing the translated audio logs on his desk.

"What's this?" He asked, lifting one brow. I couldn't make my mouth work. The words were stuck in my throat. He sighed. "Mariella, do I need to send for your sister? Do you need medical attention?"

I shook my head.

"Then please tell me what this is," he instructed.

"Audio logs from the *Aurora*," I said, my voice coming out soft and weak.

"Oh," General Rouhr said, his expression turning grim. "Any ideas on what happened to the passengers?"

"They shot themselves into space, sir," I whispered.

"What?" he demanded, rising out of his seat.

"I believe they were under the control of a Xathi queen. Maybe more than one, I'm not sure."

"Thank you for bringing this to my attention," the General said with an understanding nod. "You may go. Try to rest, if you can. I'm sure that wasn't easy for you to hear."

"Thank you, sir," I said, quietly stepping out of the room. Rest was the last thing I wanted. I didn't want to lay in silence with nothing to distract me from what I'd learned.

I wandered in the direction of the refugee bay with the intention of finding someone to talk to, when I saw

Tu'ver walk in through the doors leading to the docking bay.

Our eyes met. His expression softened for just a moment, before shifting into a look of concern.

Instantly, he moved toward me. I stumbled into his arms, tears blurring my vision and spilling down my cheeks.

"What happened?" He growled, holding me close.

"The *Aurora*," I said with a hiccup in my voice. "All those people. It's so awful!"

"You don't need to talk about it right now," he soothed, running a steady hand through my hair. "Let's go back to your cabin, okay?"

I nodded against his chest, my hands running down his arms.

My fingers came away red.

"What happened?" I yelped.

"It's nothing, really."

"It doesn't look like nothing!"

Tu'ver opened his mouth, probably to explain why his arm was covered in blood but I cut him off.

"Don't say another word," I said, getting behind him and placing my hands on his back to push him in the direction of my cabin. "I'm going to bandage you up. Don't argue with me."

"I wasn't planning on it," Tu'ver replied, shoulders shaking with laughter. Several crew members gave him a strange look as he let me push him out of the common room.

"Wow, I guess we know who's in control here," laughed on particularly ballsy crew member.

Tu'ver turned his head slightly. I couldn't see his face but did get the privilege of seeing said crewmember quickly look away and busy himself with a pointless task.

"I never get tired of doing that." Tu'ver said, obviously amused.

"Now wait till you come into my quarters," I said with a smile. "And you'll see who the real boss is."

TU'VER

Mariella pulled her chair up to the bed, sat me down in it, then grabbed a med kit from under the bed and perched next to me.

"How did you get hurt?" Her voice was calm, but her hands shook as she held the med kit on her lap.

I put my left hand on hers and used my right hand to caress her cheek. "I decided to jump out of the shuttle before it landed."

She slapped me in the chest. "What were you thinking? Why would you do something so stupid?" Fury snapped the worry clear off her expression.

"Mariella..." I said, with a smile to indicate that I had been teasing her.

Her eyes went wide, she shot me one of her sister's famous looks. "You lied to me?"

"I'm not entirely certain it counts if it's such an obvious lie. You were on the verge of tears about some scratches."

"Scratches?!" she practically shouted as she got to her feet and started pacing her room. "You call those scratches? You're *bleeding* through your bandages!"

"That's medical foam," I helpfully clarified.

"And it's supposed to close wounds," she shot back. "That is not a closed wound."

"I had just enough to get here without bleeding out." This wasn't going the way I'd planned.

"So, you could start bleeding once you saw me." Her raised eyebrow confirmed my fears. I was in trouble.

"It held during the journey back to the ship."

"And now the wounds are reopening," she said, hands on hips. "What do you have to say for yourself?"

I stared at Mariella. This was unexpected. Unusual. No one had ever been so worried for me.

"Thank you?"

It was her turn to stare at me. Finally, she just huffed and began to work on me. "Start talking." She tried to sound uncaring, but I could see her eyes darting up to my face as she began unwrapping the bandage around my arm.

I smiled at her as I took a breath, rushed the words out quickly. "The hybrid managed to escape."

She looked up at me as she cleaned the bite mark on

my arm. "The what? How?" She poured some sort of liquid on my arm, causing me to wince.

"The human... it's changing. Human isn't the right word for it anymore."

She nodded, waiting for more of an explanation.

Shame flooded through me. I'd weakened again, felt sympathy for the creature for a fraction of a moment.

And had let my guard down, potentially threatening everyone on the team.

"My shift was almost over, but the hybrid became increasingly agitated. He somehow managed to get to his feet and threw himself around the station, bouncing himself off walls, support columns, even the stairs. That's when I decided to try to retie him to one of the pipes. I untied him, he jumped me and bit me in the arm, and took off running up the stairs."

She nodded as she absorbed the story. She had done a good job rebandaging my arm, then turned her focus to my chest. "So, how did you get these?" she asked as she lightly pointed at the two chest wounds and a big cut to my leg.

"I chased him up the stairs. At the top, I saw that he had broken one of the glass doors to an office. He was laying on the ground in his own blood. I thought he had hurt himself, so I stupidly let my guard down. When I kneeled to check on him, he snapped up and cut my leg with a piece of glass. He then jumped on me and we wrestled around. He got in this cut here," I pointed to the lower of my two chest wounds, "before I was able to knock the glass from his hands. Then he scratched me with his claws here," I pointed at the other cut.

That had caught her by surprise. "Claws? What claws? He didn't have claws."

"He didn't when he first attacked us, but his changes haven't stopped. He has more crystals on his skin, his fingers turned into claws, and he started to become wilder, more feral."

"What happened after he scratched you?"

My shoulders dropped. That was the only thing that had gone to plan. "I kicked him in the chest, then again in the head, and then bounced his head off the wall. Dragged him back downstairs and tied him up, then looked for the med foam. When the others arrived, they sent me back here."

"How horrible," she murmured. "I wonder what caused him to be that way." My gut twisted. I wished I could shield her from this, but this was the reality we both lived in now.

"I think I know."

A familiar bleakness started to steal through my limbs, the cold armor my last defense.

I stalled for time, searching for words. "Can you wrap that a little tighter?" I helped her rewrap the first bandage tighter around my chest, then helped take the second bandage off. As I cleaned at it, she grabbed a suture kit and started stringing up the needle. "I've seen this—uh," I grunted as the needle broke through the skin. She mumbled a sorry as she began stitching me up.

"When the Xathi came to our world, we thought we were prepared. We assumed they would attack us by force, like they had the Skotans and Valorni. We never anticipated that they would attack our minds."

I groped for the right word to describe the feeling of having your brain bombarded by constant voices and noises you couldn't identify, an attacker that made you doubt your sense of self, reality itself.

Sensing something wrong, she paused her stitching, then leaned forward to kiss me.

Ignoring the throb in my arm I nipped at her lips, tasting her sweetness until the bitter old memories released their grip.

"It's okay if you don't want to talk about it," she said soothingly when we broke our kiss. She went back to stitching me up while I watched the movements of her small hands, the delicate motions calming me.

With a deep breath, I continued. "Some of our people were able to resist, but the ones that lost the fight started to become like that human at the station. They lost their power of speech, became primal, violent even to their friends and families." I swallowed, throat tight. "Even those that didn't become violent knew there was something wrong. They changed…"

She gasped and covered her mouth. "It's like what happened on the *Aurora*," she whispered.

"What?"

She shook her head. "I'll tell you later. You finish first."

"Are you sure you want to hear this?" I grabbed her hand, interlaced her fingers with mine.

She nodded. *The more information we have, the better prepared we are.* My first commanding officer after espionage training drilled the words into us. As an archivist, Marilla knew the value of information, no matter how horrible.

"Those of us that were losing the battle to their mind attack, we put into hospitals, schools, wherever we could to keep the public safe from them. At least, that was the plan. Some of our people were better at hiding their battle, others were better at hiding their loved ones that were losing."

Her brow furrowed. "I don't understand."

"What I'm about to tell you, no one knows. Not even the others. I…" I hesitated. My heart pounded, and my breath short and ragged. I clenched and unclenched my fists, trying to fight back my emotions. "I was one of the ones that was able to hide a family member." No emotions, just facts. "My sister, Cannira, was everything to me. She was my best friend, my confidant, and I was to be her 'sera rgel.'"

At her look of confusion, I explained. "A 'sera rgel' is a position of honor when a member of our race makes their mating bond. Most females of our race choose either their mother, their grandmother, closest sister, or closest friend, but it's always another female. Because our mother had died when I was young, my sister was going to break tradition and choose me. No one argued with her decision, because she was bright, beautiful. Perfect." Facts, I reminded myself. Cold, sterile facts. "The Xathi attacked a few weeks before her Bonding-Day."

"When I finally realized she was losing the fight, I hid her from the others. I didn't want her to be placed in an institution where our doctors were experimenting with ways to fight the Xathi mind control. I didn't want her hurt by our own kind."

I stopped talking, mentally reaching for the scraps of my old defenses. Logic. Reason. My heart couldn't hurt, because it had been cut out that day.

And still, my chest ached.

"What happened?" It was a reasonable question. But the only way I could force the words out was to become the old Tu'ver.

"The impulses were so strong, she had resorted to stabbing her own leg to make the pain block the need to attack. I offered to take her to the hospital. With my military connection, I could get her special care."

"When she smiled at me, I knew I had lost her. She told me she couldn't fight it anymore, that she had to give in or she was going to dig her own brain out to stop the voices. I never knew where she got it, but she reached under her pillow and gave me a gun. I begged her not to make me do it, but she put her hand on my leg. Her fingers were already turning into claws, her eyes paled to white. She told me she loved me, squeezed my leg, and closed her eyes." I looked away. "It was supposed to be her Bonding-Day."

Mariella had tears streaming down her face as she looked at me. I didn't have to say that I shot Cannira, she already knew.

"What did you do...after?"

"I found out that the *Vengeance* was going after the Xathi. I petitioned to join, proved myself to the crew, and..." I shrugged. "You know the rest."

She stood up and hugged me. "It's not your fault."

"I know," I answered with a gleam in my eye. "And I'm going to kill the Xathi. I will kill them all."

My heart ached for Tu'ver.

Nearly everyone on board the *Vengeance* had been touched by tragedy at the hands of the Xathi.

But this was a level of horror that I could scarcely imagine.

Suddenly Tu'ver stood, his face an icy mask. "Thank you for your assistance. I should go report in."

He leaned over to brush my cheek with his lips then strode out the door while I blinked in shock behind him.

I sat on my bed, Tu'ver's dried blood still on my hands, feeling empty in a way I hadn't felt since my mother died. I didn't know what to say because I didn't know what to feel.

I didn't understand why Tu'ver walked away like he

did. Obviously, his sister was a very painful topic. I expect reliving those memories had been horrible. I thought I'd done the right thing by hugging him, by telling him it wasn't his fault.

But he got up and walked away.

And I didn't know what to do.

I began to wonder if I even knew Tu'ver at all.

Hating the idea of staying alone in my room, I absentmindedly wandered the corridors of the *Vengeance* until I found myself in the doorway of the lab.

"Hey, Mari," Leena called. She was running some sort of simulation on her console, but I didn't look very closely. When I didn't immediately respond or move closer, Leena paused.

"Is everything okay?" she asked warily.

"I think I made a mistake," I said after a moment of pause.

"What do you mean?" Leena asked, abandoning her work to lead me farther into the lab.

"Tu'ver told me something very private and personal," I started. "I thought I reacted correctly. I reacted how I would want someone to react if the situations were reversed. But then he just got up and left."

"Just like that?" Leena asked, brow furrowed.

"He kissed me first," I admitted.

"Well, that doesn't seem too bad, does it?" Leena encouraged.

"When I say it, it doesn't sound bad. But it felt bad," I awkwardly explained. I was having unusual difficulties expressing my emotions, something I rarely struggled with. "I feel like, somehow, I let Tu'ver down."

"That doesn't make any sense," Leena said gently. "You and Tu'ver have been thick as thieves since they found us in that cave."

"I think I'm in love with him," I blurted. I hadn't meant to say it. I hadn't even been thinking about it. It just came out.

"Was that supposed to be a surprise?" Leena asked, looking genuinely confused. "Everyone knows you and Tu'ver are in love with each other. I'm pretty sure there's an ongoing bet about how long it's going to take one of you to admit it."

"Seriously?"

"Probably," Leena amended. "Even I saw something in the way he looked at you when he carried you out of the cave."

"This is horrible," I said, putting my face in my hands.

"What?" Leena blurted. "How is this horrible? You love him. He loves you. Everyone knows you love each other. What am I missing here?"

"Tu'ver and I were finally at a place where we could

express our feelings toward one another just in time for me to prove that I'm not worthy of him." I hung my head, feeling like an inconsolable child.

"That's the stupidest thing I've ever heard," Leena exclaimed.

"But it's true," I said, blinking away the tears that had welled up in my eyes. "He trusted me with something that he's never trusted anyone else with and somehow, in some way, I failed him. I don't even know how I did it, but I did. I don't know how to fix it."

Even as the words tumbled out of my mouth I knew they sounded illogical. But it was how I felt.

Hollow and hopeless and wrong.

"That still doesn't make any sense to me," Leena said, rubbing my arm in an attempt to comfort me. "I don't know what sort of advice to give. You know I don't have a lot of experience in this department. Axtin and I are both blunt. If we have a problem we say it. Then we yell. Then we make up," she said with a wicked smile that ordinarily would have made me laugh.

Now I could only stare at her. How could I fix something when I didn't know what the problem was?

"I have something that might cheer you up!" Leena said brightly. She hooked her arm through mine and led me to the console. "The data you brought back from Glymna was incredible. I'm pretty sure that gas you found is N.O.X. I'm running simulations using a variety of blood samples. It's behaving exactly how I would imagine the early stages of the illness started."

"Blood samples?" I asked, distracted from my circling thoughts. If Leena was focused on a project, who knew what she'd be capable of...

"Willingly given by refugees," she reassured me. "But that's not the point. Mari, if this gas is what caused the mutation, I can reverse engineer an antidote. We might finally have our cure!"

The world suddenly spun around me.

One of the few certainties I allowed myself to believe was that I was going to die young.

I'd based the entire way I lived my life around that knowledge. I had made peace with it.

What does one do when a constant suddenly changes?

"Amazing, Leena." I meant it. The work she'd done was incredible. But I couldn't even bring myself to smile.

"Doesn't that make you happy?" Leena said, her brow wrinkling with concern.

"Yes!" I said quickly. "It's just a lot to take in. I..."

It was too much.

"Mari, are you okay?" Leena asked, taking one slow step toward me like she was afraid I would bolt.

"I'm not sure," I said, shrugging my shoulders

slightly. "You thought shutting out all of your emotions could protect you."

"Yes," Leena said, confusion in her voice. "But I don't know why you're bringing that up now." I could tell from the tightness of her smile and the slight flare of her nostrils that I'd offended her. She was showing restraint by staying calm. I'd tell her how much I appreciate it when this numbness went away.

"I did the opposite," I replied.

Leena now looked more confused than angry.

"I made sure I felt the biggest emotions I possibly could. I chased after them. I wanted to feel everything all the time so that when something truly awful happened, I wouldn't be afraid. But something truly awful has happened and I feel just as vulnerable as I would have been otherwise." I didn't know if I was talking about the *Aurora*, the Xathi, or Tu'ver.

"That makes about as much sense as me hiding from emotions, I guess," Leena said with a sympathetic smile. "We're really messed up, aren't we?"

"I guess we are," I said with a weak smile. "I'm going to go."

Leena frowned. I could tell she wanted to ask more. Even I was aware of how out of character I was behaving, but I didn't know how to explain anything.

I didn't even want to try.

I left the lab and walked slowly back to my room

in a trance. I would come back and see Leena when I was feeling more like myself. I just needed some time.

It was too much too fast.

Falling in love with Tu'ver then realizing how little I really knew about him, learning about what happened to the people on the *Aurora*, Leena finding a potential cure, and the constant fear that the Xathi could attack at any moment.

It was too much.

I felt too much too deeply. All at once. I think I broke something inside of me.

Halfway to my room, I realized I didn't want to go to my cabin. I changed course, heading for the library instead.

As soon as I stepped into the room, the sinking feeling in my chest felt worse. I turned around and left immediately.

As I continued to wander the halls, I half-hoped to see Tu'ver.

But how would that make any of this any better? I still didn't know what to say to him, what had gone wrong.

Normally he'd be the first person I'd want to tell Leen's news of a potential cure. But he'd acted so oddly as he walked away. Cold, remote.

A stranger in a familiar body.

I tried to think logically. On a normal day, what would I be doing now?

My stomach gurgled, and I realized I hadn't eaten all day. I slowly made my way to the mess hall but took nothing.

I wanted Tu'ver's cooking.

I wanted Tu'ver's smile.

Really, I just wanted Tu'ver.

But that wasn't going to happen.

TU'VER

I woke alone.

As I should be.

It was safer for everyone that way.

Koso, I didn't care about everyone.

It was safer for Mariella that way.

The decision had become clear last night as I sat in in the dark. To avenge Cannira, to protect Mariella, the logical course of action was to resume my old nature.

Cold, distant. And alone.

I wouldn't fail Mariella. She would stay safe, but I couldn't let the darkness touch her shining light.

Even mine. She didn't know what I was, what I'd trained for. And that was for the best.

It was the right choice. The logical one.

Surely the ache in my chest would fade with time.

I checked my wounds as I prepared for the day. My flesh was almost completely closed, self-healing circuitry activating. Marilla had done a good job.

I should tell her, check on her after sharing the horror story of my past.

No.

I should leave her alone.

Against my every instinct, I turned away from her quarters to report to General Rouhr for new orders.

"Sk'lar's and Karzin's teams are fine," Rouhr checked his datapad. "Vrehx and Daxion are working with some of the humans on learning how to use the defensive systems that are still operational. Relieve either Axtin or Sakev from your little project."

Right. The hybrid. That would be a practical use of my time.

He thought about it for a moment. "Send me Axtin. I can use his help to start working on forging more weapons for this hand-to-hand fighting idea you srell came up with."

He smiled when he called us srell, so that meant that he actually liked the idea.

I gave him a quick salute and a "Yes, sir," and headed out. The idea of Sakev and I monitoring the creature together was not my favorite, but I could live with it. I headed down to the shuttle bay, made sure my gear was in proper order, and fired up the thrusters.

Leena and Mariella passed through the shuttle bay on their way from the labs, too engrossed in their conversation to look up.

Good. It was better this way.

The trip back to Kangefi Wetlands was relatively boring. I did spot some Xathi chasing Luurizi in the plains east of our forest, but nothing of immediate danger to the ship.

The Wetlands were a marvel to me. While we did have wetlands on my home world, they were nothing like here. Back home, our wetlands were fields of water with plants growing out of them, never getting taller than my waist.

Kangefi was an entire island of jungle with pockets of water-filled land. When I had used the computer at the station to do some minor research, I had found reports describing the creatures living on the island.

There was a man-sized beast with scales and hair that seemed to swing in the trees. There were creatures that were reportedly like the tiger on the ancient human home world, whatever a tiger was. But this one was twice the size and varying shades of grey, black, and yellow.

There was something they called an anaconda that stretched nearly thirty feet in length and was reported to be able to swallow a full-sized adult human with ease. They had discovered nine different species of birds, another dozen or so species of insects, and over three hundred species of plants within the jungle. They had also discovered a species of spider that seemed to be able to spin webs between their legs and fly from one end of the island to another.

I repressed a shudder. The idea of a flying spider was honestly the scariest thing I had ever imagined as a child, and it was apparently real on this planet.

Koso spiders.

I waited until I was in sight of the station to call.

"Xathi prisoner cell one! How can we help you?" Leave it to Sakev to make a joke out it.

I kept my voice level. It wouldn't do to let Sakev think he had gotten under my skin with his juvenileness. "Sakev, it's Tu'ver. Tell Axtin to get his gear together and meet me outside the station. Rouhr needs him back at base."

"Aww. How come the General never wants me to do something?" his voice came back, feigning disappointment.

"Think about it, Sakev," I said as I started to land the shuttle.

"Good point. I'll tell Axtin." His voice became serious. "Welcome back, Tu'ver. It's changed."

"Understood," I said as I touched down. I set the Scrapper into stand-by mode, grabbed my gear, and walked out. We had made our landing zone a section of an outcropping approximately twenty yards from the station.

Axtin emerged from the station, his hammer strapped to his back and his bag of weapons hanging from his left hand. He waved at me and picked up the pace.

"Glad you're back." He clasped my arm, all his usual humor gone. "When you left yesterday, Vrehx estimated only thirty to forty percent of its body was covered in crystal. Now? The whole damn thing, and I don't think it's just a cover anymore. I think its skin has transformed completely to crystalline like the Xathi. Not as thick, but definitely there."

His jaw tightened "Its eyes are closed shut, but it follows you around no matter where you go, like it can still see you. And to top off the creepy factor, it makes a weird noise every now and again, totally randomly. Drives me crazy." He shook himself, pulled his focus back to the immediate. "What does Rouhr want?"

"Time for you to make some weapons."

He brightened up and clapped his hands together loudly as he let out a Valorni howl. "It's about time I get to make some new toys. I have an idea for some miniature versions of my baby, and maybe some ways to modify her so she can have some electrical pulses when she hits."

His enthusiasm at the idea of manual labor was

unmistakable. He loved building and improving things, which made me wonder what he would have been if the Valorni weren't always fighting something. He slapped me on the shoulder and wished me luck, then headed towards the scrapper.

I returned the sentiment and headed into the station to the second floor where we had made a modified cage for the creature in one of the old offices. Sakev sat at a desk using the console, his blaster was only a few inches away, its barrel conveniently pointed towards the creature.

He looked up at me and smiled. "So, what brings the intrepid assassin back to the creature bin?"

He was flippant and a joker, but not an idiot, proven when he quickly backpedaled.

"Apologies. In all seriousness though, what brings you back? It's not your shift for another twelve hours."

"Axtin was needed." And I needed distance from the ship, Mariella. "Tell me what's happening."

He cocked his head and took a deep breath. "A whole lot of things as well as a whole lot of nothing." Sakev got up from the desk, making sure to grab his blaster as he did. "He just sits there. Sometimes he makes a noise for a few seconds, sometimes he makes it for nearly a minute, but otherwise he just sits there. That's the nothing. The 'something' is that he's changed, a lot."

"Yes, Axtin told me." I walked up to the makeshift cage. The office that we had commandeered to be used as a cell had been empty except for the desk and console Sakev had been sitting at. We took those out, found some piping in the Aurora, and modified the door and window so that it couldn't get out, but we could see in and get in if necessary.

It sat in the corner of the room, like Axtin and Sakev said. It seemed to take notice of me, because now it decided to get up and stand just like me. Every move I made, it mirrored. I said a random word, it tried to imitate me.

Was this a further evolution of the process? Did a new person in the room trigger a new reaction?

Just as I had had enough and was about to turn away, it made a high-pitched whine. The sound only lasted a few seconds, but it was painful. It then looked at me and sat back down. As I moved to the side, its head followed me. I turned back to Sakev to see him staring at me.

"What?" I asked.

"That was a new sound," he said. "Usually, his noises were just annoying. That one was painful."

"I wonder why the change." I examined it again, cataloging changes.

The skin was now completely covered in crystal, and it looked much thicker than it had before. His eyes were interesting. Using the scope from my rifle, I could still see the eyes where they were supposed to be, but the crystalline skin had grown completely over them, like built in goggles.

Its hair had become stiffer as if it also was taking on crystalline properties.

But the sounds were most interesting to me.

I grabbed a metal cup that had been left behind and took it to the cage. I began dragging the cup back and forth over the bars, the clanking noise loud and obnoxious.

"Hey!" I could hear Sakev yelling behind me. "If I had wanted to listen to bad noise, I would have stayed with Axtin and had him explain his rekking hammer to me. What are you doing?"

The creature had done nothing. It just sat there, staring at me. "A small experiment. I wonder if it can hear…" The creature began emanating that loud squeal it had done before, this time louder.

Doing my best to plug my ears, I walked over to Sakev and leaned in close. "Did it make any noise like that before?" I shouted.

"No!" Sakev shook his head.

"Srell." I turned back towards it. "SHUT UP!" I yelled.

Surprisingly it did. Was it some latent human memory of the meaning of the words, or the force and tone behind them, the lower resonance different from the clanging on the bars?

"Wow. Why didn't I think of doing that?" Sakev asked.

This thing confused me. I wasn't sure what it was and what it was up to, I just knew that something wasn't right. For the next hour, it stayed silent. Sakev and I spent the time trying to read up on the information left behind in the station and speculating on the hybrid.

I hated speculation without data. And we simply didn't have enough to make informed projections. Hopefully Rouhr would soon approve Leena to travel here. We'd sent her video of the creature, but surely as a scientist she'd rather make her observations in person.

I could escort her, make sure nothing happened to her. Nothing that would upset Mariella.

No. I couldn't let my thoughts go there.

Pushing aside the distraction, I noticed the hybrid stood near the cage door. Not facing us, its head pointed up to the ceiling.

A low hum rumbled through the room.

Sakev and I exchanged looks.

"Son of a rekking dog!" Sakev said. "What the koso is it doing now?"

"I think," I started. My hand itched with the sudden need for a weapon. "I think it's calling for help."

Sakev's eyes went wide. He ran to the console and opened a channel to the *Vengeance* and Axtin's scrapper.

I took a position by the window.

They blended in well with the jungle, but not so well I couldn't see them.

A horde of hybrids.

Coming to free their new hive mate.

Right through us.

MARIELLA

"Bring me the cathartic wipple snap," Leena said without looking up and extending an empty hand in my general direction.

"Nice try, but I know that's not a real thing," I said. The corner of my mouth twitched. That was as close as I could get to a smile.

I'd spent the day in the lab. There wasn't much I could help with, but I felt like I should be there as she tried to construct the cure that would save our lives. Plus, I think she liked having an assistant to boss around.

More than once, I suspected she'd deliberately asked me to bring her the wrong thing just so she could make me do it again. I didn't mind though. I knew that was just her way of trying to get me out of this funk.

I barely slept last night. I couldn't remember the last thing I had to eat. I didn't feel hungry or tired. I didn't feel anything really. I didn't even feel excited as Leena narrowed in on a likely cure. I simply didn't feel.

"You would have fallen for it a few hours ago," Leena replied.

"Sorry to ruin your fun," I said, walking closer to her console. "Any progress?"

"The antidote I've made is working well with the infected blood samples," she said, Yet, it didn't sound like a good thing.

"But?" I prompted.

"Unless I test on live, fully infected subjects I won't know exactly how well it works," she explained.

"I doubt any of the refugees would be willing," I said, mostly joking.

"If I were able to offer something by way of financial compensation we'd have a line out the door," Leena huffed. "Not that I would ever do that," she added quickly.

I swear, no one understood how difficult it could be to have a mad scientist for an older sister.

"So, you have a general idea of how it could work but we won't know for certain until we—"

"Test it on ourselves," Leena finished.

"Sounds great," I said blankly.

"What exactly have we got to lose?" Leena replied.

She had a point.

I sat in silence while she continued working. The thought of injecting an untested serum into my body to combat an illness that, until about three days ago, we knew nothing about should have scared me more than it did.

Leena wouldn't test anything if she had any reason to believe it would kill us quicker than the illness.

The worst-case scenario was something I was already prepared for.

"Do you think I should go talk to him?" I asked, breaking the silence.

"Tu'ver?" Leena asked, still absorbed in her work.

"Who else?" I replied.

"Well, since you're both devoid of all emotion, now would probably be the best time to talk about difficult subjects," she answered.

"I genuinely cannot tell if that was sarcastic or not," I said.

"Honestly, neither can I," Leena replied.

"Tu'ver isn't devoid of all emotion," I argued, feeling a bit offended on his behalf. "You just don't give him enough credit."

"You're probably right," Leena admitted much to my surprise. "Go talk to him. It can't possibly make you feel any worse."

"That's one way to look at it," I shrugged. "Okay, I'm

going to go find him. I'll be back in a little while."

"Good luck," Leena called to me distractedly as I left the lab.

Tu'ver wasn't in his room, the mess hall or any of the common areas.

I went to the docking bay, thinking that he might be working on one of the Scrappers, but he was nowhere to be found. I found the docking coordinator, a stocky Valorni and asked if he knew where Tu'ver was.

"He's already gone back to the Quake station," the coordinator informed me.

Something snapped in me then. All the emotions I'd been unable to feel came rushing back like a tidal wave.

Tu'ver shouldn't be at the Quake station.

Not with that…what did he call it?

That hybrid creature.

Not with his injuries unhealed.

Suddenly the bay erupted as a swarm of Valorni, Skotan and K'ver soldiers rushed past me.

"Go! Go! Go!" Vrehx yelled. "Shuttle three is prepped. They're holding them off, but the Quake station won't hold for long!"

What?

Icy fingers gripped my spine.

The Quake station. Where Tu'ver had gone.

While the soldiers boarded I slipped to the other side of the shuttle and found an access panel.

I worked it open frantically and then froze. Was I really going to do this?

Jump into the unknown?

The answer was immediate.

I was going to Tu'ver.

I was going to make this right, no matter what.

I slid into a small alcove screened from the rest of the shuttle by a thick bulkhead just as the main doors clanged shut.

"Lifting off!" someone shouted as the shuttle rose up. "Primary thrusters on!" In my nook the air crackled from the wave of intense heat. "Secondary thrustors primed and... go!" We shot forward. I didn't make a sound as we flew - at this speed it would only be a few minutes flight.

I breathed a sigh of relief.

They wouldn't turn back now even if they found me.

I gripped the handle of the alcove, knuckles white as the shuttle touched down.

"The hybrids are everywhere," Vrehx growled. "Clear a path."

Shit.

Tu'ver was not going to be happy when he saw me.

"Secure the station, then destroy the horde!" Vrehx yelled as the doors to the side and rear opened and the soldiers exited before I even knew what was happening.

The feral shrieks of the hybrids filled the air and suddenly, the realization came to me.

I was alone in the shuttle.

And I didn't know how to close the doors.

Slowly I crept from my hiding space and peered out the side doors. My mouth dried as I caught my first glimpse of the hybrids. Tu'ver had said it was changing, but I hadn't realized the entire island had been overrun by the creatures.

Unlike the rest of the human survivors I'd met, I was the only one who'd never come against the Xathi. I'd studied them in the archive, but that didn't, couldn't convey the sheer horror before me now.

These were humans, had been human once, but they were in various stages of a terrible transformation. Skin and hair covered with crystal, blank eyes didn't seem to slow any of them down as they swarmed against the warriors who fought to clear a path to the besieged quake station.

Before the wedge of the soldiers, one by one hybrids fell.

With every breath another hybrid fell, often even before the warriors reach them.

Tu'ver must be perched somewhere, picking them off with his rifle.

The vice around my heart eased a fraction. Right now, he was alive and fighting back.

Surely, I could do something to help.

Wriggling forward to the cockpit I examined the instrument panel.

The shuttle wouldn't have any weapons on it, or the men wouldn't have abandoned the advantage of strafing from the high ground.

Tu'ver had tried to teach me how to pilot a Scrapper. It couldn't be much different than a shuttle, right?

I studied the controls, chewing my lip as from the corner of my eye I watched a contingent of hybrids break out towards the shuttle.

Crap.

There were so many buttons. Navigating something like this required skill and experience, not a half hour of casual instruction.

The guttural cries of the hybrids came closer, echoing through the empty shuttle.

Wildly I stabbed at the panel, hoping blind luck would let me hit the right combination to close the doors.

Instead the shuttle jerked and lifted, rocking wildly.

I clung to the controls, grateful that at least the hybrids had been taken by surprise and knocked off.

Now, if I could just figure out what I did…

By trial and error, I managed to work out a simple plan: Rotate until the back of the shuttle was to a clump of hybrid, check that none of the men of the *Vengeance* were in the way, and hit the primary thrusters.

The screams behind me weren't human, not anymore. Still, they would haunt my sleep, if we made it out of this alive.

Rotate. Check. Fire.

By the third iteration the hybrids apparently decided the shuttle was too much of a threat to ignore.

They swarmed, attacking from every side. Desperately I tried to lift higher out of their reach, but a smooth take off was still years behind my skill. The shuttle lurched and bucked with every leap in altitude until finally I was knocked out of the pilot's seat and onto the floor.

I grabbed for anything I could get ahold of but with no one at the controls the shuttle kept tipping. My hands slipped along the smooth exterior looking for purchase. I kicked my legs, hoping they would catch on something.

They didn't.

My fingers jammed into the edge of the door, holding me for just a moment as I dangled in midair.

The hybrids shrieked at each other, circling eagerly below me.

The craft lurched again.

And I fell to the waiting horde of monsters below.

TU'VER

There was no way around the bitter truth.

The fight with the hybrids was wearing us down. They weren't as strong as the Xathi, but they were fast and completely fearless.

They also seemed to be of a hive mind like the Xathi, their coordination too quick and fluid to be basic telepathy or standard communication.

It'd be useful information if we survived.

When the hybrids first came out of the jungle, Sakev shot the captive four times, the final shot taking the head off. "Can't risk it at our back."

"Do you hear me complaining?"

We quickly made our way downstairs and barricaded the door and windows. We had just finished pushing a heavy table against the main door when the first wave of hybrids reached us, pushing back the door.

Sakev responded by putting his blaster through the space between the door and its frame and proceeded to empty his first clip. We got the door closed and stepped back.

It was nerve-wracking to be inside that station as the hybrids beat on the doors, beat on the windows, and seemingly beat on the walls, trying to get in.

"Get to the top, try to pick some of them off. I'll hold them down here if they get in," Sakev yelled as the first window broke.

I put a round through an unlucky hybrid's head before I answered him. "No. You won't be able to hold them all on your own."

"I'll take out as many as I can, then blow the stairs behind me," he said as he put another hybrid down with a great shot.

"And by blowing up the stairs, how do we get down?" I asked as I shot another hybrid. Then a second window broke. Sakev shot through that one. We looked at one another, each of us grabbed a grenade, flipped the pin, tossed them outside, and ran up the stairs.

We were knocked off our feet as the grenades went off but regained our footing and made it up the stairs. I glanced out the window to see the shuttle arriving.

"Incoming!" I yelled, pointing. Sakev looked, nodded, and opened fire down the stairs. We spent the next two minutes emptying clip after clip into the hybrids below before we heard answering gunfire.

Within another minute, the rest of the team burst through the doors securing the exit.

"Move out!" Vrehx yelled. We grabbed our gear and ran. I took the stairs two or three at a time, rushing out of the station.

"Srell!" I cursed as I caught my first good look at the horde. It was the band of humans that had confronted us when we first brought the women to the *Aurora*. Or at least, it had been.

"Find a defensible spot," Vrehx snapped.

My sniper's heart wished for the roof of the building, but the station had never been built for defense. It was too easily overrun.

A small tree gave me the height I wanted, and I got to work, clearing a way for the rest of the team to engage.

Spray of crystal after another filled my scope as I picked them off, one and another and another blurring into a sea of targets.

Until something broke my focus.

"Did you leave a pilot behind in the shuttle?" I asked Vrehx through my commlink.

"No," he replied.

Who was flying it? Rocking, it rotated towards us until I caught a flash of wide, terrified eyes above the control panel.

Koso.

Mariella.

The screams of the charred hybrids cut the air and I allowed myself a brief smile. It was a clever plan, if she'd had any training on the shuttle.

My fingers cut into my palms as I watched her, then returned to my own work. Sealed in the shuttle she was safe enough.

Then she rotated a bit more, and I saw the side doors gaping open.

Still, she was in control. I couldn't let myself slide.

Another target, then the next, the press on the team easing as the hybrids redirected their rage to the shuttle.

Suddenly the small craft bucked higher into the air, and before I could move Mariella hung from the opening, frail legs kicking for purchase.

Srell.

As Mariella fell into the middle of the hybrid horde all thought ended, and instinct took over. I fired off the last two shots in my rifle's clip, dropped it, and pulled out my knives.

A hybrid managed to tangle itself in Axtin's legs,

taking him down to a knee. I threw a knife into the creature's back and used Axtin as a ramp, running up his back and leaping into the air. At the apex of my jump, I pulled another blade and screamed as I fell into the writing mass.

Mariella lay sprawled on the ground, a hybrid sniffing at her body.

A hybrid arm hit me in the back of the head while a claw reopened one of my chest wounds. I responded with a quick upward stab to the jaw, its convulsing body taking a knife with it, and a slash to the one that clawed at me.

Its hand flopped on the ground like an out of water fish. I punched the one-handed hybrid and kicked another one away from me.

The one that had been sniffing Mariella snarled, then opened its slavering jaws. My arm snapped forward, the knife embedded itself to the hilt in the thing's skull. As it fell, I drew a blaster and fired a shot at a another in the crowd, opening its stomach.

Belly wounds, shots to the knee, point blank shots to the head, every round in my clip found a home. I pulled the trigger, and when nothing happened, I bashed my target in the face, then popped out and slipped in a new clip. I punched it again in the face, then shot it in the heart.

My wounds throbbed, a small alert in the back of

my mind, but the only thing that mattered was that I got to Mariella and kept her safe.

After I had no more ammunition left, I retrieved my knife from the sniffer's head, and used that.

When a giant hand caught my wrist with a loud crack, I looked at my new opponent without recognition, determined to get out of his grasp to continue my mission.

"Easy. We're friends, remember?"

I blinked, looked again at my hand, the knife held microns from Axtin's throat. His hands were raised, eyes as wide as I had ever seen them.

Daxion held my wrist.

Slowly the rage faded, too many breaths passing before I loosened my grip on the knife. Daxion caught it as I let go and stepped away.

"My apologies, Axtin."

No other words were necessary.

If he had something to say, he'd say it, as would I.

But later.

I fell to Mariella's side, brushing the hair way from her face.

To my shock, her chest rose and fell.

Breath.

Life.

Vrehx said something, the voices of the others all

faded away as a new mission grabbed me, just as urgent as the previous.

Get Mariella to the medbay of *Vengeance* immediately, and the hell with any repercussions.

MARIELLA

I hadn't thought there could be anything more painful than getting caught up in a rockslide.

Apparently, I was wrong.

My whole body throbbed like a single exposed nerve. My head felt like it weighed fifty pounds and I was certain every one of my bones was bruised. Even my eyelids ached when I tried to open them.

"Everything is alright, dearest," Tu'ver's soothing voice drifted into my ears, the only part of me that didn't hurt. "Don't try to talk or move just yet."

"What happened?" I croaked out, throat dry. Cool fingers pushed my hair off my forehead and a steady hand gripped mine.

"You nearly stopped my heart, that's what," Tu'ver said dryly.

Slowly, everything started coming back The Quake station, the swarming hybrids, the shuttle. I fell right into the center of a horde.

Curious, I craned my head to look at my body, despite the ache. My bare arms were crisscrossed with superficial scrapes and bruises. I was sure the rest of my body bore similar scratches.

Tu'ver must have noticed what I was looking at, for he spoke up. "Almost all of your marks will vanish in a few days. We were able to treat you quickly." Sweet man. The thought of permanent scars hadn't even crossed my mind.

"Is everyone okay?" I asked, looking back at Tu'ver laying beside me in the medbay bed.

"Everyone is fine." He stroked a finger along my cheek with a featherlight touch, pitch-black eyes mesmerizing. "When you fell from the shuttle you provided a large enough distraction that allowed us to completely overwhelm them."

There was something he wasn't telling me, something hidden in his voice.

But I'd ask later. Now I just reveled in being alive, and with him.

"Glad I could help," I said, my voice fading in and out. With the gentlest touch I could imagine, Tu'ver took my chin in his hands and turned my head so I had to look at him dead on.

"When I lost sight of you in the rockslide, I had never been more afraid in my entire life. I swore I'd never let anything like that happen again. When I saw you fall from that shuttle, I felt myself die. I thought I'd lost you forever."

"I'm so sorry I put you through that," I said, unable to stop the tears from welling up and spilling over.

"It wasn't your fault," Tu'ver soothed. "But I still don't understand what you were doing at the Quake station in the first place."

For a moment, I'd completely forgotten as well. When memory struck, I sat up to face him, but was immediately hit by a wave of pain that forced me back down.

"Easy." Tu'ver placed a hand on my shoulder so I wouldn't try to move again. "The analgesics are still working through your system. You'll be fine shortly but give them a chance."

"I couldn't find you, and I didn't know what was wrong between us," I blurted out, tears burning my eyes. "When Vrehx said the station was under attack, I couldn't stand it. Couldn't stand by wondering if you were going to come home, if everything between us was gone forever even if you did return."

I turned away, but he pulled me to his chest, fingers stroking my hair. "Then it's doubly my fault." He pressed a gentle kiss to my forehead. "All I wanted was to keep you safe. From the war, from my past." He paused. "From me."

"Idiot," I choked out, running my hand up the side of his face. "When you're by my side I'm happy. I don't need you to keep me safe, I need to be with you."

His body stiffened at my touch. "You don't know what you're saying, Mari. I'm not a good man. I've done terrible things."

Time to play dirty. "Would you ever hurt me?" I asked with wide eyes.

A muscle in his jaw jumped. "I would kill anyone who tried."

"Then don't leave me again," I murmured, my lips brushing his throat.

"Mariella," he groaned into my hair. "I love you more than anything. And no force in the universe will ever change that."

"You love me?" I asked, my cheeks aching from the smile that overtook my face.

"Of course," Tu'ver said as if it were the most obvious thing in the world. "I think I loved you the moment I saw you in that cave."

I pushed back against his arms to look at him. "I love you, too."

Tu'ver gently wiped the last traces of tears from my face before leaning down to kiss me. Instead of letting the kiss end, we pulled each other in deeper.

Slowly, we shifted until we were pressed up against each other. I placed a hand on his chest, feeling the steady beat of his heart.

One of his large hands traced a line from the slope of my neck, over the curve of my shoulder and down to my hips before making the slow journey back. I continued to kiss him, opening my mouth in invitation. The hand I'd placed on his heart drifted down towards the very noticeable hardness in his trousers. A low growl tore from his lips when I made contact.

His hand found my breast, barely concealed under the thin material of the med bay gown I was wearing. He slowly stroked a thumb over my nipple. I sighed against his mouth.

"Are you sure you're not too sore for this?" he whispered.

"I'll survive," I moaned back, pressing my breast into his hand.

The first time we made love in the canyon, it was primal. We surrendered to our need and our lust in an explosion of exquisite pleasure.

This time was different.

Tu'ver was slow and deliberate, exceedingly careful as he removed my med bay gown and eased me onto my back.

"The door," I whispered.

"Koso." With a quick movement he rolled out of bed,

lay his hand flat on the wall until his circuits flared. "It won't keep out anyone with an emergency, but no one will wander in," he reassured me. "Now, where was I?"

With a wicked grin he lifted my ankle, kissing down the length of my leg, then climbed on the bed before switching to the other. Kissing and stroking up and down my thighs his touch making me dizzy with sensation until without a pause his breath hit my core.

"Tu'ver," I squirmed, suddenly uncomfortable. "You don't have to-"

"Taste you? You couldn't stop me." His tongue dragged through my folds, then lapped at me, sucking my clit in rhythm as his fingers pierced me.

Sparks crashed through me, the intensity driving me off the bed but with one broad hand splayed across my belly he held me down, held to his mercy until I shattered, writhing above him.

As I caught my breath he rose, smiling broadly, and quickly stripped. Before I could admire the view, he lifted me into his lap, my legs bent to either side of him.

"Still doing alright?" He whispered, nibbling the shell of my ear.

In answer I rocked my hips towards him, grinding on his hard length. Laughing, he lifted me, strong fingers working my hips until I was position over the broad head of his cock.

He did all the work, lifting me up and slowly

lowering me onto him. A deep shudder of pleasure engulfed my entire body. We'd gone so quickly the first time, I hardly had a moment to truly appreciate how well-endowed he was. Now, I was able to marvel at how perfectly he filled me. I let my head loll onto his shoulder. I kissed wherever my lips could reach.

He listened perfectly to every cue my body gave. With each slow thrust, he pushed deeper and deeper. My already sensitive breasts grazed his chest as he lifted me up and down. I rocked my hips, a silent plea for more. He tightened his grip on my hips, holding me suspended just above his lap for him to thrust up into. It was like I weighed nothing at all.

I let my hands roam over his body, leaving a trail of gentle scratches down his back. He groaned against my mouth, our tongues dancing together as we pushed each other closer to the point of release. Every nerve in my body zeroed in on the building intensity at the apex of my thighs.

Within moments, I was trembling around Tu'ver as I reached my peak.

Tu'ver gripped my hips, plunging as deep into me as he could as he found his own release. We clung to each other for a long moment, shaking and panting.

Eventually, he lifted me off him, laying me back down on the bed. A light sheen of sweat covered my body but I didn't mind.

"How do you feel?" He asked. I knew he was talking about my injuries but that was the farthest thing from my mind now.

"Wonderful," I sighed. Tu'ver chuckled as he laid back on the bed. He pulled me in close to this chest.

"I'll ask you again in a few hours when you're too sore to move," He chuckled.

"Worth it. Completely worth it," I affirmed.

"Don't think your incredibly effective methods of seduction can distract me from the real issue here," he said. I tipped my head back to look at him, brow furrowed.

"No more heroics," he said with mock sternness. "You're the worst planner I've ever met."

"That's why I drag you along every time," I explained. "I need you to pull me out of trouble when my plans backfire."

"This is a terrible arrangement." His laugh rumbled deep in his chest. I pressed myself closer to the sound. "But I wouldn't change it for the world."

"I promise not to launch myself off canyons or fall out of shuttles anymore, okay?" I sighed melodramatically.

"That's all I ask," Tu'ver replied, running his fingers through my hair. "Although, I think we should take another trip to Glymna once you've recovered."

"I'm recovered!" I insisted. "I could go right now." I

tried to sit up but was met with a wall of soreness that forced my right back down.

"What am I going to do with you?" Tu'ver sighed, shaking his head.

"Whatever you want," I replied with a wink.

"Careful now," he warned. "I don't think you could handle another round." But even as he spoke, his hands were already roaming over my body. Goosebumps rose over my skin. His clever fingers dipped between my legs.

"Try me," I dared.

He obliged.

TU'VER

"Hey! You sleeping with your eyes open?"

I looked up to see Axtin staring at me at the table in the mess hall, actual concern on his face.

Srell him for breaking my memories of last night's time with Mariella. "Apologies, I was thinking. I see I let my guard down," I said as I took a drink of my Mandemorian ale, by far the smoothest drink I had ever had.

Axtin sat across from me, setting down a ridiculously overloaded tray of food. "Are we at peace with the universe and no one told me?" He chuckled a bit as he bit down on a big strip of meat.

It was a terrible sight to watch him eat. "You must really allow me to cook for you one of these days. I know you don't have that sophisticated of a palate, but this," indicating his cacophony of food mixed together on his tray. "This is a disaster."

He laughed, stuffed several bites in his mouth, and chewed with his mouth open, purposely trying to disgust me.

However, his joy was short lived as he choked on his food and started coughing it up. I laughed at him as he pounded on his chest and tried to breathe.

When his green face got darker in color, I stopped laughing, jumped over the table, and helped him clear his airways.

As he sat there, nearly hyperventilating to get air in his lungs, I went back around to my side of the table, trying not to laugh.

"If you two children are done trying to kill one another, I was wondering if I could join you." Vrehx stood at the end of the table, a grin on his face.

I gestured for him to take a seat as I reseated myself.

"We were just talking about food when he tried to impersonate a dying person," I said. I refilled my cup with ale, then offered the pitcher to the others. Vrehx declined, but I poured a cup for Axtin, who was still coughing.

We sat in relative silence, Axtin's lingering coughs the only thing that broke that silence. Finally, once Axtin was done coughing, and back to eating, Vrehx started the conversation.

"Let's start with what happened at the Quake Station. I want to know why you left us like that."

Really? That was the question he wanted answered? Fine. "Mariella was hurt. I had to get her here to medbay."

"Protocol is that battlefield injuries are triaged on the shuttle first, then transported. What were you thinking?"

"I was thinking that the Scrapper was faster than trying to carry her to the shuttle."

He stared at me for a few moments. "Why?"

I looked at him quizzically. "Mariella was injured, the Scrapper was faster, I did what I had to."

"But, the Scrapper had to be hard to fly with two people on it, especially at the cliffs on the shore line," he pressed.

"What do you want me say, Vrehx?" The familiar anger flickered through my veins. He was pushing the conversation in a very stupid direction.

He stole a vegetable from Axtin's plate, took a bite of it, grimaced, and laid it on the table. "Not cooked right. Tevo must be on duty tonight." He turned his attention back to me. "I want you to tell me the truth. Why did you act the way you did?"

"Srell your protocol." I stood up, ready for a fight. "I love her, and I wasn't going to waste any time getting her back here to keep her safe. Does that make you happy?"

Vrehx just stared, Axtin took a bite of the ribs on his tray. Neither of them moved until Axtin finished chewing, then they looked at one another, looked back to me, back at one another, back to me, then back at one another before bursting out in laughter.

"I told you he'd lose his mind if you pushed him," Axtin said between loud guffaws.

"You were so right," Vrehx agreed. He reached into his pocket, took out a coin, and gave it to Axtin. "You won the wager."

Smiling, Vrehx turned back to me. "Oh, sit down. We were just having some fun with you. You know damn well that Axtin and I would have done the same had it been one of our women."

Still angry, I sat down slowly. They had really been messing with me?

Vrehx continued talking. "You're a terrible person to your friends when something you value more is in danger, you know that, right? Not that that's a bad thing, but ...it's a bad thing. Do you even remember nearly decapitating Axtin?"

"It wouldn't have been a decapitation, just a minor throat slice," I argued.

They both looked at me wide-eyed, then chuckled. "He's back to calm," Axtin smiled. "Thanks for not cutting my head off, although, your 'minor' throat slice would have killed me anyway."

I grudgingly agreed with him.

"So…you love her?" Axtin asked.

While it was something easy enough to admit to myself, admitting it to them was more difficult. Although, I'd already done that in my little tirade a few minutes before.

Koso.

"There's just something about her that soothes me, makes me feel something new. Different."

"Aww, he's adorable." Axtin cooed as he nudged Vrehx.

I kicked him under the table, bringing a shout from his lips. He rubbed his leg, but that ketonsin smile of his stayed on his face.

"Well, as much as I'd love to keep talking about our relationships," Vrehx started, his demeanor growing serious. "We need to talk about our newest problems."

"The hybrids and the recordings Mariella found on the *Aurora*," I guessed.

"Let's start with the hybrids. Leena has told Axtin, who then told me, that you've had some experience with them?" Vrehx asked.

"In a manner of speaking. They tried a mental attack on my planet before resorting to a more traditional one. It drove too many of my people insane, and in the process, they began to change."

"Change how?" Axtin asked.

"The same way we've seen so far with the humans. Their minds gone, eyes changing, skin changing, it was nearly the same. Many of my people think that it was the enhancements, the augmentation we wear, that saved us." I proceeded to tell them about what happened on my planet. I left out my sister's story, but everything else I had seen and heard was enough to get the point across.

"How do we deal with them?" Axtin asked after absorbing it all.

"On my world I believe the Xanthi grew tired of waiting for their hybrids to conquer us and sent a squadron of attack ships." I shrugged. "So, for now, I'd suggest the same way we've dealt with them already. We kill them."

He shook his head. "Sorry, I meant...is there a way to save the humans?"

I had nothing to say to that. As far as I knew, nothing our doctors had tried had made a difference.

Vrehx didn't look pleased with my non-verbal answer, but I think he had the same answer as me.

"Do you think that was what happened to the people of the *Aurora*?" Axtin said. "They were starting to be

controlled and were able to fight it off enough to open
the air locks?"

The idea of being mind controlled, of having to kill
yourself to fight it off obviously bothered the big man.

I couldn't blame him.

"I have to think so," Vrehx said. "I wish I knew more.
We are going to have to go back, and probably soon
before the Xathi get there and occupy it."

"How much of it do you think is operable?" I asked.

Both looked at me, but I could see them considering
the idea as I continued talking. "Think about it. No, it's
not very well defended, but we could potentially use parts
of the *Aurora* to fix the *Vengeance*. That would let us get
off planet and back to our own corner of the universe."

"Now that's an interesting idea. We could get back
home," Axtin agreed. Frowning, he mused. "Do we want
to, though?"

Vrehx turned to look at him. "What do you mean?"

"We've each found someone. Would we leave them
behind to return to war? Would we ask them to leave
their home to come with us and live in a war zone?"

I was truly disappointed to realize that I hadn't
thought of that. "Would it be any different than what
we were doing right now, though?" I wondered aloud.

"No, but yes." Trust Axtin to be complicated in his
answer. "We're already living with the constant threat

of Xathi invasion, and this planet is slowly being turned into a warzone, so everyone here is already dealing with it."

Vrehx nodded, and I scowled, not liking where this was going.

"Here we only have *one* Xathi ship to deal with, and we've already injured a sub-queen. I haven't seen an actual queen yet, so there is a real hope that once we eliminate the Xathi here, then this planet is safe again."

The words were bitter. "So...what do we do?"

"Evaluate options," Vrehx decided. "And for now, appreciate what we have."

What we have.

None of us had ever expected to find a moment of peace in our war with the Xathi.

But somehow, we'd each found more. Someone to spend our lives with.

I thought of Mariella, of her sleepy smile as I'd slide out from bed this morning.

Whatever happened, she'd made it all worthwhile.

EPILOGUE : MARIELLA

"You're one hundred percent sure this won't kill us, right?" I asked Leena as I watched her pipe the liquid that could cure us into a syringe. It didn't help that the serum was inky black in color.

Not logical. Not reasonable.

But it still gave me the creeps.

"There's no such thing as one hundred percent in science," Leena replied. The slight waver in her voice gave her away- she was nervous, too. "There is always the potential for human error."

"Thanks, I feel so much better now," I quipped.

"If it doesn't work, I can always try again," Leena said with a shrug. The gesture was meant to appear casual, but her shoulders were too stiff to be convincing.

"Unless this kills us," I blurted. Leena gave a hollow laugh.

"Well, look at it this way. If I'm right, we're cured. If I'm wrong, it isn't our problem anymore."

"Wow, that's bleak," I laughed dryly. "Who's going first"

"I am," Leena declared with a stiff nod. "If it doesn't work, I'd rather it be me than you."

"Now I want to go first," I argued. Leena gave me a stern look as she shrugged out of her lab coat and pushed up the sleeve of her grey shirt.

"Okay," she said, taking a deep breath. She didn't give herself a moment to hesitate or change her mind. She stuck the needle in her arm and pushed the plunger down. I watched the black liquid enter her. For a moment, it turned the veins closest to the needle dark as well. The sight of it made me feel a little nauseous.

I really wish I'd gone first.

"It's cold," Leena said with a shiver as goosebumps rose on her skin. "But so far, that's it."

"So, you don't feel like you're hurtling toward the end of your life?" I ventured.

"If I were, I'd think you'd know it," she replied. "Let's wait a few minutes before injecting you though."

A few minutes stretched into over an hour. Each time I insisted it was okay, Leena asked for just a little bit more time to be doubly sure nothing would bad would happen to me. I practically had to wrestle the syringe from her hands.

"You don't know how to do it," she insisted, clutching the syringe with both hands. "You'll probably rupture your own vein."

"Then you do it," I sighed impatiently. "But for goodness sake, Leena. At this rate, the illness is going to kill me before you let me test the cure."

"Sometimes it takes a while for side effects to materialize," Leena said defensively.

"Do you want me to go get Axtin? Because I'll tell him you're trying to control everything again," I threatened.

"You're such a tattletale!" Leena groaned. "Do you know what he did last time when he thought I was getting back into old habits?"

"No, what?" I asked, already amused. If it was something Axtin did, it was almost guaranteed to be a good laugh.

"He lit a fire in our room," she huffed. "I had to sit still for a full thirty seconds for him to put it out."

"That's one way to do it," I said, holding back laughter.

"So, don't tell him about this," Leena insisted. "He'll probably try to make me meditate while he pours acid on my desk."

"Give me the serum and my lips are sealed," I grinned.

"You're *such* a little sister," Leena grumbled as she disposed of the syringe she'd used and replaced it with a clean one. She piped in another dosage of the black serum. "You ready?" She asked, chewing on her bottom lip.

"No, I need to think about it for another hour," I said, rolling my eyes. She glared at me.

"Sorry for showing concern about dosing my sister up with an untested serum meant to cure an illness ninety percent of medical professionals don't believe exists," she snapped.

"I'm sorry," I said. "It's just so fun to tease you."

"You and Axtin are going to drive me to an early grave," Leena sighed. "Hold out your arm."

I did as I was told. Something about seeing the vial of black liquid and the needle pressing against my skin suddenly made me nervous.

"It doesn't hurt right?" I asked in a quiet voice. Leena smiled kindly.

"Just a little pinch," she answered. I flinched when the needle poked into my arm. The serum entered my veins, briefly turning them black before disappearing beneath my skin.

I shivered a bit. Leena was right, it made me feel

cold all over. She withdrew the needle and disposed of it.

"That was unpleasant," I said with a shudder. "But I don't feel any different. I take that as a good sign."

"For now," Leena nodded.

"Now what?" I asked, rubbing my arm where the needle pierced me.

"I'd like to keep you here for a little while and observe you," Leena said.

"I'm not a lab rat!" I scoffed.

"Yes, you are," Leena chuckled. "I am too. Now sit and concentrate on everything you feel happening in your body." I hopped up onto a lab table.

"I feel a little hungry," I started. "I probably should have gotten more sleep last night. My lower back itches—"

"You know that's not what I mean," Leena sighed as she took a seat in a chair across from me.

"I already told you I don't feel anything," I said. "I don't know what you expected."

"Something helpful," Leena replied.

We sat in a strange silence for at least an hour, occasionally punctuated by awkward attempts at conversation. I could tell Leena was trying to balance her analytic chemist side with her sister side. The more she scrutinized me, the more nervous I felt.

At long last, she broke the silence.

"I've got to go," Leena said, looking at the timepiece on the desk. "Vidia's started running a makeshift school for the kids on board. Calixta should be almost done with her lessons."

"Tu'ver wants me to meet him in his room anyway," I said, sliding off the table. "I think he's making dinner."

"You'll let me know if you feel anything, right? Even if you don't think it's something let me know," Leena reminded me for the ninth time as we walked out of the lab.

"I will," I replied.

"Or at least write it down," she implored.

"I will!" I repeated. "Try not to worry too much," I said, giving her arm a squeeze before we parted ways.

I could smell Tu'ver's cooking before I reached his door. I didn't need to knock, he'd given me access to his cabin whenever I wanted. I spent most of my nights here. His bed wasn't as big as mine, but it felt more comfortable.

Plus, he had made a bookshelf. For me.

"Smells good," I sighed as I walked into the tidy cabin. "Is it fish?"

"If that's what you want it to be," he said with a wry grin.

"That's an unsettling answer," I said, looking at the frying meat with a critical eye.

"Jeneva said it won't kill us if we eat it," Tu'ver said as he sprinkled the filet with seasoning.

"Oh, that's a relief. I was hoping to only put one potentially toxic substance in my body today," I laughed dryly as I took a seat at the small table. Tu'ver's expression shifted to one of seriousness.

"Are you well?" he asked, sitting down at the table across from me. He reached over the surface to pick up my hands.

"It went well, I think," I replied. "The serum was cold. But other than that, Leena and I both feel fine."

"So, I'm going to have a very long life with you?" Tu'ver asked.

"It looks that way," I smiled. He leaned across the table to kiss me tenderly.

The possibly-fish cooked quickly. I helped Tu'ver plate it alone with sides of greens in a dressing that smelled fruity and one of the bread-like rations from the mess hall. Tu'ver poured us each a glass of something pale blue and bubbly that tasted like berries. I eagerly dug in once we were seated.

"Whatever this is, it's delicious," I exclaimed between bites.

"So how does marriage work?" Tu'ver asked suddenly, not looking up from his plate.

I nearly spat out my drink.

"What?" I sputtered.

"That's what you humans do when you fall in love, yes? Have a marriage?" he asked, looking perplexed by my reaction.

"Two people get married if they want to spend the rest of their lives together," I supplied. I felt a blush rising in my cheeks.

"Let's do that, then. How does it work?" He looked at me, his face filled with such a genuine curiosity that I couldn't help but laugh.

"There's aren't really any rules, not anymore."

He frowned. "In my people's culture, this was a most important affair, tied about with tradition and ritual." A shadow crossed his eyes, and I knew he was thinking of his sister.

"Let me think." I chewed my lip, pulling to mind what I'd read about the traditions from Old Earth.

"It could be a rather long process," I explained. "First there is an engagement. That can last for as long as the couple in question wants it to. During that time is when the couple plans the ceremony. The details of the proposal, engagement, and wedding varied from couple to couple."

"Does the female plan the wedding?" Tu'ver asked, brow still furrowed.

"That's not a strict rule," I amended. "That was how it was most commonly done on Earth. Some elements of the tradition carried over."

"And what is a proposal?"

"On old Earth, the groom presented a token of commitment to the bride, usually in the form of a ring," I continued. "Though that isn't a strict rule either. The bride can propose, too. And the token doesn't always have to be a ring."

"There are far too many variables," Tu'ver nodded thoughtfully. "So, all I must do is present you with a token and then the process begins?"

"Yes," I giggled. "However, most brides like to be surprised," I said with a wink.

"Ah," Tu'ver said, his face lighting up with understanding. "In that case, forget I asked anything at all."

"I'll get right on that," I laughed.

I felt giddy through dinner. Once Tu'ver and I cleaned everything up, we stretched out on his bed. He picked up a datapad containing a book we'd chosen from the library. Every night we took turns reading aloud to each other. Tonight, was his turn.

I laid my head on his chest, listening to his deep voice as he read. Soon, it was difficult for me to keep my eyes open. I knew I would be asleep soon. I always fell asleep when he read.

"Hey," I said softly, reaching up to kiss his cheek. "I love you."

"I love you, too, Mariella" he whispered softly. "Always and forever."

My last thought as I drifted off to sleep was how happy I was as I heard that.

And how happy I would be.

Forever after.

LETTER FROM ELIN

I hope you liked spending the time with Tu'ver and Mariella. It was great fun letting him show a bit of emotion, even it he's not entirely comfortable with it :)
Next up, everyone's favorite prankster, Sakev!

DR. EVANGELINE PARR *lost it all when the Xathi attacked Fraga. When she's asked to establish a clinic in the devastated town of Einhiv, she jumps at the chance to help.*

The only problem? A smart ass, joking Skotan warrior. He's a terrible patient. Impossible. Refuses to take anything seriously.

Until they're caught in an explosive situation, and a new side of him emerges.

Protective.

Efficient.

And very intriguing.

SAKEV JOINED *the Skotan fleet after an... unusual career. The ghosts of his past have mostly subsided against the ongoing struggle to keep up with the Xathi attacks and their new hybrid weapons.*

Mostly.

He never expected a tiny human female to break through his carefully constructed facade.

But his past pales against the mystery of the war they're fighting. And when the enemy changes get again, keeping Evie safe becomes more than just another mission.

It's the only mission he cares about.

XOXO,

Elin

S akev

"Is it too much to ask for one of these trees to come to life?" I looked from mossy trunk to mossy trunk for some sign of movement.

"Why would you want that in the first place?" Axtin, our resident heavy hitter, replied.

I'd think he'd be the first to jump at the chance to fight one of the sentient tree beasts that roamed the forest.

"Because as much as I love our daily nature walks," I started, practically feeling Vrehx bristle at my description of our routine patrols, "I'd like to do something useful."

"How is fighting one of those skrell walking trees useful?" Vrehx asked.

I'd gotten under his skin. It was an art form I'd perfected by this time. One day, it was going to get me punched in the face, but it wouldn't be the first time.

"Maybe it's not useful, but it's entertaining." I grinned back.

"So, you're whining because you're bored?" Vrehx sighed. "Sorry the Xathi war isn't *entertaining* enough."

"Don't get me wrong. Fighting the Xathi, saving people, and all that good stuff are plenty entertaining. We just don't do any of that very often," I remarked. "You can't expect me to believe that the best we can do is to walk along the same forest paths every day."

Alright. It wasn't the same paths over and over. That would be stupid. But we'd covered so much of the surrounding area it all looked the same.

Aside from a few isolated incidents, we'd barely made a dent against the Xathi invasion. The massive, crystalline, insect-like creatures had been slowly choking the life out of this planet. The humans who inhabited it were ill-prepared for something like this.

When we'd fallen through the rift in space and landed here, we became their only hope. And the best we could do was stroll through the woods near our ship, the *Vengeance*.

It wasn't enough, but it looked like I was the only one who'd admit it.

"Do you want to be on galley duty tonight? If so, keep running your mouth," Vrehx seethed.

I was having fun now. The others in our strike team were silent, but I could see by the tightness in the corners of their mouths and the rigid way they held their shoulders that they were trying not to laugh.

"I don't mind helping out in the galley. Snipes is a good guy, though his cooking leaves much to be desired." I shrugged.

Axtin snorted.

"Silence," Tu'ver said sharply. He'd stopped moving entirely.

The witty remark I'd planned died in my throat.

I gave Tu'ver as hard of a time as I gave everyone else, but when he stood still like that in the field, even I knew it was best to shut my trap.

"What is it?" Vrehx asked in a hushed voice.

"Movement to the east. Whatever it is, there's more than one." Tu'ver lifted his impressive rifle and peered through the scope. I knew it had a ton of fancy upgrades and mods, not that Tu'ver would ever let me try it out.

"There's a refugee camp somewhere nearby," Axtin said. "Maybe it's them."

"Let's check it out," Vrehx ordered. "We'll offer aid if we can. Is that a satisfactory use of your time, Sakev?"

"It's not taking down a sentient tree, but I guess it'll do." I grinned.

If there were people nearby, fleeing the Xathi, of course I wanted to help them. Since we were no closer to actually defeating the Xathi, helping people was the next best thing.

"I'm going to get a better vantage point." Tu'ver quickly scaled a tree and disappeared into the canopy.

It's hard to believe someone that big could move like that. K'vers weren't as heavily built as Skotans, but Tu'ver and I were of similar heights and builds.

I definitely outweighed him, though. A branch that supported him would snap under me.

It wasn't long before Tu'ver's voice crackled through our radios.

"Not humans. Hybrids. Four of them. Hunting for something."

"Didn't you say there were refugees in the area?" I asked Vrehx, who nodded. "That must be what they're hunting. We have to take the hybrids out."

Tu'ver dropped out of the tree and landed silently beside Vrehx. Under different circumstances, I would've been equally impressed and creeped out. He moved way too quietly.

"Do we have a location on the human refugees?" Vrehx asked.

"They move each day," Tu'ver replied. "They weren't far from here yesterday, but who knows where they are now."

"What does it matter?" I asked. "The hybrids will find them eventually, no matter where they are. We have to take them down."

"We don't know that the hybrids are hunting the refugees," Vrehx replied.

"What else would they be hunting?" Axtin asked.

"Us," was Tu'ver's grim reply. "It must be driving the Queen mad knowing we're here but being unable to find us."

The *Vengeance* had the most sophisticated cloaking device I'd ever seen. I didn't fully understand how it worked, but it was extremely effective. We'd been here for quite a while, and the Xathi still didn't know where we were.

"Is that less of a reason to grind them into dust?" I asked, though I was largely ignored.

I guess that's what I got for pissing Vrehx off. Fair enough.

While the others went back and forth about the best course of action, I pulled a small gadget out of my pack. It was something I'd been working on to beat the boredom of stagnant ship life.

It was a standard scanner that measured heat signatures, but I'd amped it up. It could scan farther and in more detail.

In theory, at least.

I'd never actually tested it.

I quietly powered it up and scanned the surrounding forest. The good news was, it worked like a charm. Heat signatures lit up the tiny screen, mostly small creatures of the forest.

There was a large clump moving strangely. That had to be the hybrids.

To the south, much closer than I would have liked, was another large group. The refugees.

The hybrids were moving towards them quickly, but before I could tell the others, the device threw sparks and the screen went black. It was totally fried.

My mind was racing. By the time Vrehx and the others decided on a course of action, it would be too late. They'd never believe what I saw, now that my scanner was busted.

It was only four hybrids, according to Tu'ver. They would be nothing but warm-up exercise.

I could get there, take them out, and get back in no time. The refugees would be safe, and my strike team wouldn't be at risk.

That would be a win-win scenario.

"I'll handle it," I said over my shoulder as I took off into the forest.

"Sakev, get back here! That's an order!" Vrehx yelled, but I wasn't going to stop now.

The hybrids were not stealthy movers. I heard them long before I saw them.

The first one never saw me coming as I fired a shot through its skull. The other three wailed and hissed, throwing themselves at me.

As we fought, I noticed how they clicked and chirped to one other. Their attacks were more coordinated than they had been the last time I fought them.

It was unusual for the Xathi to create slaves with any level of intelligence or autonomy. It was definitely worth mentioning to Rouhr.

I felled a second one. This would be over in no time.

I was already planning how I was going to rub this in Vrehx's face. It'd probably earn me galley duty for a month, but it'd be worth it. And I really did like hanging out with Snipes.

One of the hybrids paused long enough to let out an ear-shattering screech. I'd heard it before. It was calling for reinforcements.

There must've been other groups nearby, groups Tu'ver hadn't seen.

"You're going to get us all killed!" a voiced yelled

from behind me. The rest of my strike team emerged from the trees to join the brawl.

"You weren't supposed to follow me!" I shouted back, but my words were drowned out by the sound of approaching hybrids.

Lots of them.

"Skrell!"

We were overwhelmed. They were everywhere, more than I could count.

"Call for an evac!" Tu'ver shouted over the chaos.

I barely heard Vrehx shouting into his radio. A hybrid scrambled toward me, but I didn't have enough time to react.

It practically exploded, just feet away from me, as Axtin's gigantic hammer smashed into its side. Shards of crystal flew everywhere. I howled as a thick shard embedded itself deep in my arm.

"Strike team two is coming," Vrehx called out. "We just need to hold out until then."

There was a gash on the side of his head. Blood trickled down his face, blending in with the red of his skin. Tu'ver was firing with his off hand, his good arm bent at an odd angle.

This was my fault.

We pulled together in a clump, firing and lashing out in any way we could.

The hybrids were smarter than they'd been before,

but thankfully, most of them hadn't developed a thick crystal coating yet.

That was our only advantage.

One shot from a blaster would bring them down.

I heard the sound of a shuttle from somewhere above us. Strike team two descended on ropes, joining the fray with vigor. With our efforts and ammunitions doubled, we were eventually able to beat back the hybrids.

Those that didn't fall scurried back into the forest. No doubt the Xathi Queen already knew what transpired.

I looked around. No one had escaped unscathed, but we hadn't lost anyone, either.

This wasn't supposed to happen. I should've known they would follow me. It's a good thing they did, but they weren't supposed to get hurt.

The humans had a saying for this. I'd heard Axtin's human mate say it once or twice.

No good deed goes unpunished, or something like that.

Vrehx stood off to the side, talking into his radio. I walked up to him, but before I could open my mouth, he cut me off.

"Say even one word, and I will leave you here for the hybrids to pick apart."

I shut my mouth and nodded.

I deserved that.

EVIE

"Dr. Evie, I'm telling you! I'm sick to my stomach. I think I'm going to die!" The tiny voice came from the floor of my office.

I used the term "office" very loosely. In reality, it was just a small corner of the refugee bay, bordered by dingy curtains pulled together from who knows what or where.

I didn't mind, though. It was nice to have some semblance of normalcy.

I peered over the edge of my desk that doubled as an examination table. It was nothing more than a sheet of metal laid over two empty barrels.

One of my regular patients, a child named Calixta, was curled up on the floor, writhing in agony. It was a bit she played at least once a week, each time more dramatic and life threatening than the last.

By now, I suspected she knew she couldn't fool me, but she always tried. It was like a game, and I'd be lying if I said I didn't find it amusing. I looked forward to her visits.

"Calixta, if you're tummy is hurting as bad as you say it is, I might have to take out your appendix!"

Calixta peered up at me through a curtain of dark hair.

"That's fine," she said, completely straight-faced.

I couldn't help but laugh.

"What are you trying to avoid?" I walked around my desk to sit on the floor beside her.

I'd tried to liven the space up with a dusty old rug, but it didn't help much. I could still feel the cold of the metal floor seeping into me.

"Miss Vidia is teaching fractions, and I'm terrible at them," Calixta mumbled.

Vidia, the former mayor of Fraga, the city that I once called home, had taken it upon herself to continue the education of the children who now lived aboard the *Vengeance*. I couldn't think of anyone I admired more.

"You're always going to suck at fractions if you keep running away from them." I tucked a strand of hair away from her face.

I didn't know exactly what happened to Calixta's parents, but they weren't here. Same for many of the other children that had made it to the *Vengeance*. We, the adults, all lent a hand in looking after them.

"Why do I even have to learn them? It's stupid." Calixta lifted her head from the floor and sat up.

"Leena had to learn fractions."

Leena was my ace in the hole when it came to Calixta. The renowned chemist all but adopted Calixta after they survived being captured by the Xathi.

"She did?" Calixta asked curiously.

"She sure did. And so did I. Leena couldn't be a

chemist and I couldn't be a doctor if we didn't learn fractions."

Before Calixta could reply, the curtains of my office were pushed aside as a Skotan soldier entered.

I quickly glanced at Calixta to make sure she wasn't frightened.

The aliens rarely came into the human area. Some still felt uneasy around them, but Calixta didn't seem to mind. In fact, Calixta treated the aliens with more kindness and respect than most humans I knew.

"How can I help you?" I asked.

"General Rouhr requests your presence in the med bay at your earliest convenience."

I couldn't hide my surprise. General Rouhr ran things on the *Vengeance,* but I'd never met him. I didn't think he knew I existed.

"Calixta, please go to class." I gave the child an affectionate pat on the head. I helped her to her feet and ushered her into the main bay.

"And I'll be checking with Miss Vidia to make sure you attended!" I called after her as she ran off.

"Lead the way." I gestured to the soldier. He nodded.

As we made our way through the refugee bay, most of the people paid us no mind. Some stared, still not used to seeing aliens on a regular basis. Others outright sneered at us.

Even though we were alive because of the *Vengeance*

crew, some people continued to hate aliens on principle. Those were the people I treated in my office. They refused the clearly superior care in the med bay simply because it wasn't human.

I didn't agree with their small-mindedness, but it gave me something to do.

I'd never been to the med bay, but I had to admit I was excited to see the sort of technology used for treatment. I heard it was run by a fully functioning AI that was decades ahead of the AI we'd developed on Ankau. I wondered if it was advanced enough for me to talk shop with.

"What does General Rouhr need me for?" I asked once we left the refugee bay.

"A strike team got into a scuffle out in the forest. Some hybrids got the better of them."

I'd heard talk of hybrids. They're horrible creatures, caught somewhere between human and Xathi. They're mindless slaves to the Xathi Queen.

Most of the humans were kept in the dark about what was happening outside the *Vengeance*. After what they'd been through, many preferred it that way.

Vidia often spoke with General Rouhr, offering knowledge of the towns. I got all of my information from her.

The med bay was a flurry of activity. Every bed was

filled with soldiers in various injured states. One of them, a K'ver, definitely had a broken arm.

General Rouhr, a battle-worn Skotan, stood in the center with his fingers pressed into the bridge of his nose.

"You asked for me?" I approached cautiously.

"Evangeline Parr?" he asked, and I nodded. "Good. The med bay AI isn't performing to its full capabilities. We deactivated several functions to conserve power, since it wasn't being used. Ironically, now we need those functions. You have the most advanced medical training of anyone on board. I was hoping you'd be willing to pick up some of the slack until the AI is fully functional once more."

"Of course." I looked skeptically at the wounded soldiers. "But my training is for humans."

"How different can it be?" General Rouhr said with a slight smile. It took me a moment to realize he was making a joke. "Your help is appreciated."

"Where should I start?"

I was anxious to work. Plus, this was a chance to learn more about the aliens I now lived alongside.

"Some of my crew has already started patching up the minor injuries," General Rouhr explained. "If it's all right with you, I'll have you start on our most severely wounded."

He pointed to a bed in the back of the med bay.

Another Skotan was twitching in pain, though clearly trying not to. His skin was more vibrant than General Rouhr's, likely indicating a younger age, though he was not lacking in scars.

"I'm on it." I hoped I didn't sound nervous.

The injured Skotan was huge. Well over six feet, if I had to guess, and very well built.

I almost didn't notice the thick crystal shard protruding from his arm. It looked like the spike went clean through the muscle. It must've been incredibly painful.

"Who let a human in here?" the Skotan said through a wince.

"General Rouhr asked me to assist with some injuries. I'm Dr. Evangeline Parr."

"Rouhr must want me dead if he's letting a human work on me," the Skotan hissed.

"My mortality rate is one of the lowest on the planet, so you needn't worry." I forced a tight smile onto my face. "Looks like someone met the business end of a hybrid."

"And here I was, thinking I just ate some bad stew," the Skotan snapped.

I didn't react. Pain made people lash out. I'd learned not to take rudeness personally.

I picked up the data pad mounted next to the bed

and pulled up his medical information. Apparently, his name was Sakev.

I gasped at the sheer number of times he'd been admitted to the med bay. This guy was either the clumsiest solider in existence or had some kind of death wish.

"Okay, clearly you aren't new to this." I set the data pad down. "Let's get right to it, shall we?"

"No, I really want to keep the crystal embedded in my arm. I think it's pretty," the Skotan, Sakev, snapped again.

I stepped away from the bedside, trying to hide my annoyance.

The medical supplies were organized by species. I quickly located an unused syringe and a vial of fast-acting painkiller. I filled the syringe with the largest dosage I could give.

With any luck, it would put him to sleep as well as numb the pain. This was the most exciting case I'd gotten since I'd come aboard.

I wanted to get it done in peace.

"This is more for me than it is for you." I quickly jabbed him with the needle.

"What was that?" He looked between me and the needle sticking out of his good arm.

"Just a little something for your pain and my peace of mind," I said with a sweet smile.

His eyelids began to flutter closed. I watched his vitals as the painkiller carried him into a state of unconscious bliss.

"That's why you shouldn't be an asshole to your doctor," I huffed as he drifted away.

SAKEV

Oh, what a wonderful feeling, I'm happy to say.

Wow. What had that woman given me?

That human song kept playing in my head over and over again. I couldn't stop it. At least my arm didn't hurt anymore, or my leg, or my back, or my head.

Do they make that stuff in canisters?

I shook my head and tried to clear my thoughts. Whatever she had shot me up with messed with my head. I didn't like it.

I noticed that she had taken the shard from my arm and placed it on a tray near me. Wasn't it blue before?

It was...I remembered.

When we fought the hybrids, the crystals on their bodies were blue, like the Xathi soldiers, but this crystal taken out of my arm was almost clear now. There was hardly any blue left to it. Weird.

She smiled down at me.

I drooled. These meds were *great!*

Then I felt a new sensation, like something biting

me. I looked down to see her sticking my arm with a needle, pulling thread through the new hole she'd just put in me.

"Oh, I was hoping you'd leave that hole there. Gives me a new pocket to hide things."

The look on her face was priceless. I chuckled.

She pulled harder on the thread. It hurt.

"Okay. If you do have to stitch me up, can you at least make sure the scar looks good? Some sort of design maybe?"

"Sure. How about a pretty flower?" Her face was serious, but her tone was light.

I liked her.

She had an ethereal beauty to her.

And she was humorous.

"So the 'asshole' gets a flower?"

Vrehx's voice came from my right. "If it stops him from talking, give him a bouquet of flower-scars."

He wasn't happy with me.

I couldn't really blame him. I had acted rashly and irresponsibly. I hadn't taken the hybrids seriously enough, and it has cost all of us.

But that didn't stop me from being what the humans called snarky. "Yeah, can you stitch it like a whole, whatever he said, of flowers?"

I made my eyes wide, trying to look innocent as I

asked. It sort of worked on her, because she laughed a bit as she pulled the thread a little harder, again.

"Skrell! That hurt."

It actually did. It wasn't bad pain, it was just...irritating.

Her voice came across very condescendingly as she responded to me. "Oh, I'm sorry. Did the big, bad soldier have an owie? Should I get you another shot of medicine?"

I guess I deserved that.

I shook my head, regretting it a bit as it started to hurt a little more. "No. I shall survive."

"Good. Now shut up and stop moving, or I'm going to make a mess of the stitching."

It was one of the few times that I did as I was told. I stopped moving and just watched her. I wasn't exactly the most...how would Tu'ver put it?

Subservient?

No, that wasn't the right word. I struggled to think of it, but I was never really the type to be patient and well-behaved, not unless it was absolutely necessary. But there was something about this female human that made me just sit and watch.

Her long auburn hair was pulled back into what the other females called a "pony-tail." Not sure what a pony was, but it looked good on this one. It helped to get the hair away from her eyes...those blue eyes that looked nearly black, that's how dark they were.

And the tiny little freckles on her nose were just a bit smaller than the ones on her cheekbones. They were adorable, especially on her.

She was short, too. Lying on this bed, I was still almost face-to-face with her, which meant that if I was standing, I'd tower over her like a giant.

"And...done!" She announced as she tied off my stitches and cut away the remaining thread. "Do me a favor, okay, crystal-boy? Don't screw up my stitching. I'll be back to check on your leg and back in a few when the meds have kicked in a little more."

She moved over to Vrehx and began examining his head and shoulder.

"Take care of him for me, Madam Doctor. I don't want his woman angry at me if he's scarred," I said as she began cleaning the gash on his head.

It wasn't as bad as it had originally looked, but it was still nasty to see.

"Shut up, Sakev." Vrehx was still angry at me.

"Hey, you weren't supposed to follow me. I could have handled it, if I had a few clones of myself to send in first."

He shot me a look, the one he usually gave when I needed to stop talking.

I didn't obey.

"What's your name?" I asked the comely doctor. "I'm Sakev. I'm known as the fun one in here."

"Yeah, I can tell."

Skrell. Her coldness struck home. I tried harder.

"Come on, tell me your name. Don't make me invent one for you. If I did, you probably wouldn't like it," I teased her.

Vrehx shook his head.

I could hear Tu'ver let out a grumpy sigh. Even Axtin shook his head at me.

But still I pressed on. "What? I just want to know what her name is, so I can give her a properly addressed thank-you note."

She glanced back at me, her face serious. "You really need to just rest. You're annoying the other patients."

The thing is, though, I saw her start to smile as she turned her attention back to Vrehx and his head.

"Very well. I'll rest."

A not-so-silent *about time* came from Daxion at the far side of the room. He wasn't badly hurt, just a few small scrapes. He was helping to patch up Tu'ver, whose arm still looked terribly bent the wrong way.

I watched as she finished up with Vrehx, giving him some pain medication to take and ordering him to come back and see her that evening to check the stitching. He agreed as he went to a nearby basin, washed up, and went to help Dax with Tu'ver.

There was a sickening crack as they snapped his wrist back into place. He barely grunted, but I could see the supreme effort he put into not making a sound.

She went over to check on him, running her scanner over the wrist and arm, and ordered him into a brace, so his ligaments could rest and heal. He thanked her, and she smiled at him.

It was a good smile. Not as pretty as other smiles that I had seen, but I could see that it was genuine and held a real level of care and concern in it. As she started to look at Axtin, I decided that I had rested enough.

"Come on, give me a name. Don't make me call you something unusual like...Dot, or Flower, or Stitches." I made sure to keep my tone light-hearted. I wanted her to know that I was harmless...or as harmless as a military killing machine could be.

I got nothing from her.

"Very well. I'll have to go with Stitches then. That'll fit the stitches you put in my arm, and the stitches I'll have you in when I make you laugh."

Her reply was something from my own heart. "Let me know when you say something funny, and I'll try my best to laugh."

Everyone inside the med bay laughed. I made several different facial expressions as I nodded in defeat.

It was a good retort from her.

"That was very well done." I grinned. "I concede. I suppose I'm not as funny as I thought I was. Or maybe I haven't gotten started. But that should convince you to give me a name. Don't make me get serious about my humor."

"Oh? You weren't serious before? Okay. Give me your best shot at what you think is humor," she challenged me.

I broke out with some of my best, bringing most of team two to tears of laughter and even getting a smile out of Tu'ver.

It felt good to see him smile, but it felt so much better when I made her laugh. She visibly fought it, but she laughed several times, and that made me feel better than the pain meds did. Even General Rouhr, who was standing in a corner and monitoring things, smiled a bit.

When Stitches was done patching everyone up, Rouhr called her over.

I didn't hear everything, but I heard some of their conversation.

"He needs to stay in the med bay overnight. I'm worried about the cut to his back."

"When will he be available?"

"If things go well, he'll be back on his feet tomorrow. It's mostly a precautionary measure."

I decided to cut in. "I'm well. My back only itches a little bit." It hurt. "I'm fine."

She sucked her lips in, trying to hold back a smile.

Rouhr wasn't so nice. "Be quiet. You're lucky she's holding you in here overnight, or you'd be working in the recycling center, cleaning it up. Alone."

I stopped smiling. That was not something I wanted to do.

I *really* didn't want to be down in the recycling center. That's where everyone's...I gagged a bit.

Rouhr took advantage of my silence. "You're lucky no one was killed, and that your injuries were the only ones that were serious. If I could, I'd kick you off the team and off the ship. As of right now, you're off patrols until further notice. Let's see how *bored* you get then."

She must have seen the look on my face because she had a very sympathetic look on hers.

Later that night, as everyone else finally left, she came to check on me again. I stayed silent, letting her do her work. I rolled over, so she could check my back, which she said was good.

As she checked my arm, she smiled at me. "My name's Evangeline, but everyone calls me Evie."

She left, leaving instructions with one of the workers playing nurse to keep an eye on my arm and to get her if anything changed. She flashed me a smile as she went to check on the others.

I laid back, smiled, and closed my eyes. It had been a long day.

Madam Doctor had somehow made this war much less boring.

GET SAKEV NOW!

https://elinwynbooks.com/conquered-world-alien-romance/

PLEASE DON'T FORGET TO LEAVE A REVIEW!

R eaders rely on your opinions, and your review can help others decide on what books they read. Make sure your opinion is heard and leave a review where you purchased this book!

DON'T MISS A NEW RELEASE! You can sign up for release alerts at both Amazon and Bookbub:

bookbub.com/authors/elin-wyn

amazon.com/author/elinwyn

FOR A FREE SHORT STORY, opportunities for advance review copies, release news and the occasional cat picture, please join the newsletter!

https://elinwynbooks.com/newsletter-signup/

AND DON'T FORGET the Facebook group, where I post sneak peeks of chapters and covers!

https://www.facebook.com/groups/ElinWyn/

DON'T MISS THE STAR BREED!

Given: Star Breed Book One

When a renegade thief and a genetically enhanced mercenary collide, space gets a whole lot hotter!

THIEF KARA SHIMSI has learned three lessons well - keep her head down, her fingers light, and her tithes to the syndicate paid on time.

But now a failed heist has earned her a death sentence - a one-way ticket to the toxic Waste outside the dome. Her only chance is a deal with the syndicate's most ruthless enforcer, a wolfish mountain of genetically-modified muscle named Davien.

The thought makes her body tingle with dread-or is it heat?

Mercenary Davien has one focus: do whatever is necessary to get the credits to get off this backwater mining colony and back into space. The last thing he wants is a smart-mouthed thief - even if she does have the clue he needs to hunt down whoever attacked the floating lab he and his created brothers called home.

Caring is a liability. Desire is a commodity. And love could get you killed.

HTTPS://ELINWYNBOOKS.COM/STAR-BREED/

ABOUT THE AUTHOR

I love old movies – *To Catch a Thief, Notorious, All About Eve* — and anything with Katherine Hepburn in it. Clever, elegant people doing clever, elegant things.

I'm a hopeless romantic.

And I love science fiction and the promise of space.

So it makes perfect sense to me to try to merge all of those loves into a new science fiction world, where dashing heroes and lovely ladies have adventures, get into trouble, and find their true love in the stars!

COPYRIGHT